MT. MOURNE

DAVIDSON COLLEGE

RURAL HILL

GLENWOOD

WOOD

CEDAR GROVE

OAK LAWN

LATTA PLACE

ROSEDALE

DR. CALDWELL'S

HOPEWELL CHURCH

CHARLOTTE

CLOUD
OVER
CATAWBA

CLOUD
OVER
CATAWBA

●

●

●

CHALMERS G. DAVIDSON

●

●

●

●

Published under the sponsorship of

THE MECKLENBURG HISTORICAL SOCIETY

MAY 20, 1949

III

IV

HISTORICAL REFERENCES in this book are in accordance with published sources. The principal characters are entirely fictitious and are not intended to represent persons living or dead.

CHAPTER 1

CLOUD OVER CATAWBA

"AN OIL PORTRAIT of a chit of a girl is a vain thing and a service to Mammon."

The condemnation was no novelty in Unity congregation and the visiting minister had a right to his opinions. But Priscilla Brevard had recently returned from a young ladies' seminary in Charleston, and the coast country aristocrats entertained different sentiments.

"*Parbleu*," she bridled inwardly, "everybody in the Lowcountry isn't going to the bad place!" Out of deference to the minister's cloth and her own early training, she held her tongue, but the accusation rankled in her mind. When the visitor left she questioned her mother.

"If it was all right for great-uncle MacWhorter, and he a preacher, to sit for a portrait in New Jersey, why shouldn't I in North Carolina?" She knew he had done it because there was an engraving of the likeness published in Dr. MacWhorter's funeral sermon.

Mrs. Brevard wasn't sure. She had no spiritual scruples on the subject, but there had been no oil portraits at Rural Hill, albeit her father had been greatly blessed with worldly goods. If the truth were known, and Mrs. Brevard suspected it, her Scotch father had discountenanced portraits rather to save his shillings than his soul. To his daughter, however, the way things were done at home was good enough for eternity.

But Rural Hill in Mecklenburg County wasn't Catawba Forge in Lincoln as Colonel Jonathon Brevard had sometimes to remind his spouse. In spite of his Eldership in Unity Church, the Colonel had given his assent to the portrait. The sprinkling of Huguenot settlers who from accident or design had cast in their lot with the Scotch-Irish were occasionally more supple of spine than the stiff-backed Macs.

A curiosity to the community, the painter had arrived on horseback, with canvases, palette, and color box in his saddlebags. His studio was where he set his easel. His subjects any who would keep and pay him. No signature identified his portraits for posterity and on many canvases the busts were already lined in with only the features left blank.

"He couldn't be *a la mode*," Priscilla told her father, "or he'd go where patronage was better." But as the first of his profession she had seen at home, he was an opportunity not to be ignored.

She sat for him on the porch where the light was good. To brighten her expression, the artist related an anecdote concerning one of the Ravenels he had painted in Charleston.

"Like all Huguenot women," he concluded tactfully, "she knew how to hold her head. But her features were too irregular to permit a coiffure such as yours. You should be done by Tom Sully."

His subject flushed appreciatively.

"And if your father would permit, this portrait would be better a bit more *decolleté*. It's all the vogue with the summer people at Flat Rock." So he called Mr. Sully by his first name and had been to Flat Rock.

"I know," Priscilla said with a sigh, "they are Episcopalians. We are Presbyterians. There are enough people who'll think I'm proud having a portrait at all. No use having them think I'm fast. I was named for a lady in the Bible, you know."

After a moment she added, "If you go to Catawba Springs you won't see any low necks. That's a Presbyterian resort."

"I don't see that it's a question of religion," the artist ventured.

"Everything is a question of religion here," his sitter told him, "the clothes you wear, the books you read, even the kind of house you build."

She thought of how long she and her sisters had tried to persuade Pa to build a new house. He was well able to afford it. The iron foundry made a great deal of money supplying cannon balls to the army in the second war with England. And cotton got more profitable every year. Yet they still lived at Catawba Forge, a clapboarded log house. It had accrued with wings and L's as the family increased but it was fundamentally a pine pole structure. The white clapboards didn't conceal that fact from the neighbors. Pa had made a concession when he brought up a glass chandelier from Charleston, but the hall in which it hung was narrow. Priscilla wanted a big hall, wide and long with a circular stairway.

"I'm going to marry the man who will build me the finest house!" The vehemence of her voice startled her. She hadn't meant to think out loud, and a blush moistened her face and neck. It was a worldly, almost sacrilegious resolution. Inside, her conscience gave her a threatening twinge.

The artist said nothing. Perhaps it didn't sound so wicked to him. She wasn't really a worldling. The rouged and pearled ladies at Vaux Hall in Charleston had shocked her. Never once had she failed to get up for prayers at home or at school. She had recited the Shorter Catechism perfectly at the preacher's last catechetical examinations. Not once since she joined the church had she failed to receive her communion token. And not once since that day had she slept during the sermon, which lasted for hours both morning and afternoon. Unlike Low-country chapels, Unity's bare walls and high pulpit did not beguile away the time with visionary diversions.

"I don't think stained glass is unscriptural," she told the painter, who, not following the trend of her thought, nodded and continued his impersonal scrutiny of her features.

"There isn't a church with a steeple in the Catawba Valley," she continued. The magnificent St. Michael's on Meeting Street rose in her mind. By coast city standards, all Piedmont meeting-houses were little and mean.

"And the same thing is true of our homes," she told herself. Down in the Low-country planters had built elegant mansions for a hundred years and few were any richer today than Pa and the Grahams. There was hardly a fine house on the River, except maybe Rural Hill, though settlers had farmed here for half a century.

"No wonder we're 'back-country' in the geography books!"

When Colonel Brevard sent Priscilla to Charleston her brothers said she was off "to get a polish," but she came back with more than a veneer of change. Perhaps it would have been better had she gone to the Moravian school at Salem. Her Brevard cousins went there, and the daughters of Lincoln County's other iron-masters: General Joseph Graham, General Peter Forney and John Fullenwider. The Reverend Humphrey Hunter, minister at Unity ten years ago, had sent his daughter with those of his wealthy parishioners. It was an excellent school without social frills. Charleston education was too Anglicized for the Presbyterian Piedmont. Plain living and high thinking was a Unity motto.

"But what good are the graces," Priscilla asked, "where you can't practice them?"

The artist looked at her quizzically. "If you don't want me to put that rebellion in your portrait," he said, "you'll have to get it out of your face." Priscilla was startled by the detection and with an effort relaxed her expression to the resignation approporiate to Presbyterian virgins.

The impatient play of her brown eyes wandered from the Catawba Forge porch out over the foothills. There was nothing flat, nothing effete, about the Piedmont. The red clay of the earth burst through the green slopes at splotchy intervals. It shone like brick, as hard and unyielding as the people who forced their living from it. These were bricks without straw. Under stress they might crack, but they would never give.

Priscilla was reminded of the disapproval with which many of her parents' friends, despite their all-embracing Calvinism, regarded the moans and jerks of the plain people at camp meetings. And she remembered also how, occasionally, one of the straight-laced cousins with too tightly controlled emotions would give way to evangelism with a violence that exceeded the abandon of the Negroes.

The Catawba made a horse-shoe bend a quarter of a mile below the house. It was a red river, blood of the hills it kept alive. Probably the color washed off the

Indians, Priscilla mused. But if that were the source of
its pigment it should be black today. In place of the
papooses of the Catawbas and Cherokees, the River now
bathed hundreds of African pickaninnies.

The fancy appealed to Priscilla who yearned longingly
to romanticize her native heath. It seemed reasonable
enough. When the Catawba became the Wateree down
in South Carolina it began to change its color. By the time
it reached the Santee it was as black as an Ethiopian,
which was logical since the Low-country had owned
slaves generations before the Piedmont. She started to tell
the painter about it, but he was absorbed in his canvas.

On the banister rail lay a small volume. Priscilla reached
to get it. *The Lay of the Last Minstrel* had a double appeal.
Many of the localities depicted were familiar to the older
settlers on the Catawba, and the life it idealized was not
unlike the civilization the rising generation aspired to
achieve.

> Ten squires, ten yeomen, mail clad men
> Waited the beck of the warders ten;
> Thirty steeds, both fleet and wight,
> Stood saddled in stable day and night.
>
>   . . .
>
> A hundred more fed free in stall:
> Such was the custom of Branksome Hall.

Priscilla's father and several of his friends could boast
more black retainers than the Scottish laird had squires
and yeomen. She didn't know anyone with a hundred
horses, but several had blooded mounts and the Wilsons
were beginning to breed racers from pedigreed stock. How
easy it would be to live graciously in "Branksome's lordly

hall"—or even a Georgian mansion like Drayton Hall on the Ashley.

Priscilla was only sixteen, and her ambitions were un-hampered by house-keeping responsibilities. What a de-lightful age *The Last Minstrel* recalled. The men were all chivalrous and the women were all worshipped. Priscilla dreamed of a Howard

> . . . than whom knight
> Was never dubbed more bold in fight
> Nor when from war and armor free
> More famed for stately courtesy.

Nobody could tell him playing-cards were an invention of the devil, if they had playing-cards then, nor forbid his dancing a cotillion with his lady, if he had a mind to, till morning.

"I'll not marry a nobody," she thought defiantly, "or a preacher." They weren't synonymous, though equally dis-tasteful.

"Well, whatever it is," the artist shrugged helplessly, "you'd better get it settled. Until you've made your peace with the idea I can't go on. You wouldn't want on canvas what I see in your face." He stripped his brushes and began collecting his colors.

"Priscilla," her mother called, "if you are through for the day I want you to take a rest. This is Thursday, you know, and preparatory services for Communion begin this after-noon."

CHAPTER 2

CLOUD OVER CATAWBA

THE THREE WEEKDAY meetings leading up to Communion had pretty well exhausted Priscilla's spiritual fervor. And both sermons on the Sabbath would be long and oppressively solemn. She had almost forgotten how awesome the back-country preachers could be. One ray of hope brightened her depression.

"Thank heaven," she sighed, "Dr. McRee is preaching today."

The Reverend Dr. James McRee of Center Church, across the River in Iredell County, had been invited to aid in the observance of the Lord's Supper at Unity.

"He's more like the Charlestonians," Priscilla told her father, "than any other clergyman in the Piedmont."

"I daresay he is," the Colonel replied, "and I wish all were as happy to hear him as you and I."

To the small farmers and artisans, Dr. McRee's fastidious dress and Princetonian oratory were affectations. But to the large planters he was to their manner born.

"They've never forgiven him, have they," Priscilla remarked, "because his father invited Lord Cornwallis to dinner?"

"Well," the Colonel smiled, "he doesn't appear unduly shamed by the stigma of family Toryism. But he was a Whig himself. I believe the feeling against him derives from another failing he may have inherited from his father."

"What's that?" Priscilla asked.

"A rather marked preference for the company of personages of rank."

"Then I'm glad you've got the 'guinea's stamp', " Priscilla kissed his cheek, "in church and state."

The Elders had awarded her Communion token without question on Saturday. Privately she had some qualms about her worthiness to receive the sacrament after living amongst the worldly South Carolinians. But Colonel Brevard owned one of the two hooded pews facing the Unity congregation and it would not have done for a member of his family to be refused a token without flagrant misconduct.

"There'll be a big congregation, today," her mother said, "so remember to speak to everyone. I'm in considerable doubt about that bonnet. It may be all right for Charleston, but . . . ."

"Leave her alone, my dear," said the Colonel. He was irked that his wife should reopen a subject already debated and settled at home.

For the three preparatory services, the congregations had been small. Today was Priscilla's actual debut after her year's "finishing" in the Low-country. All of Unity's first families would be present. Priscilla named them over:

Her cousins, the families of General Joseph Graham of Vesuvius Furnace and of Captain Alexander Brevard of Mount Tirzah. The Robert Johnstons of Oak Grove, with the finest brick house west of the Catawba. The household of Captain John Reid, proprietor of Catawba Springs and owner of the other hooded pew in Unity. Captain James Connor's people from Poplar Grove plantation. And the straight-laced Knoxes. She remembered the time a hornet stung Precentor John Knox on the nose while he was lining the hymn. Though his eyes streamed

water he read without a quaver until the minister merci-
fully pronounced the benediction.

So infrequent were Court Weeks and General Musters
in Lincoln County that going to meeting was almost a
social necessity. Although tainted with Episcopacy, the
Forneys of Mount Welcome and the Burtons of Burton
Place would probably put in an appearance.

"Will there be people I should remember from Center?"
Priscilla asked. Since her grandfather Brevard and his kin
had originally settled in Center she knew that everyone
from that congregation was cousin somebody unless obviously beyond the pale.

"Doubtless a few," her father said, "but there'll be many
more from Hopewell." Priscilla's mother's people lived in
Hopewell, and while they were not as prominent in
Presbyterianism as her father's, they devoutly loved a
public gathering. It was not uncommon to use the ties
of kinship to get in an extra Communion. Hopewell was
an older congregation and had a much larger church, but
Unity was rapidly approaching it in wealth, and the same
blood ran in the veins of both.

In spite of the solemnity of Communion Sunday the
prospects for seeing and being seen gave Priscilla a
quickening of anticipation. His daughter's obvious eagerness put Colonel Brevard in a reflective mood.

"You modern young people," he said, "have a great
many advantages unknown to our day. These French-
speaking daughters and Latin-spouting sons are something new in country churches."

"*Naturellement, mon pere,*" Priscilla agreed prettily.
"This is 1815. But you had two brothers at Princeton,
you know."

"Nassau Hall was a good college," he replied. "It and old Queens in Charlotte educated about all the doctors, lawyers and preachers we had. Most of the boys had to stay at home and work."

The third generation in the Catawba Valley was beginning to come into a gentler day. The first two had few refinements. Without exception the pioneers had worked with their hands. While North Carolina was still a colony, servants had been rarities in the Piedmont.

"We had more indentured help than we did Negroes," Priscilla's father told her. "Orphans were bound out to families able to keep them. Not many men went to Charleston to buy blacks. I guess your mother's grandfather Samuel Wilson was about the best fixed man on the River."

"And your father's Uncle MacWhorter," added Mrs. Brevard not to be outdone in in-law concessions, "the best educated." The Reverend Alexander MacWhorter had been President of Queens, patriotically rechristened "Liberty Hall," during the Revolution. When Cornwallis occupied the town he lost his library and his love for Charlotte. The College never regained its standing after his flight. "What we girls learned," Mrs. Brevard continued, "we got from our mothers. There weren't any boarding schools for females."

"Not even Salem Academy?" Priscilla queried unable to conceive of a pre-Salem Piedmont.

"Salem wasn't opened to boarders," her mother replied. "Only Wachovia girls were admitted there until after the turn of the century."

The sedate Moravian school had become almost a hall mark of respectability for Piedmont misses. In addition to Priscilla's Lincoln County contemporaries, it was patronized by Mecklenburg Connors, Lattas and Lowries and by Iredell Osbornes, Davidsons and Allisons, all of whom were related by blood or bond to Priscilla.

For the past several decades the boys had flocked to the state universities at Chapel Hill and Columbia, greatly relieved to be freed from the necessity of four years exile in New Jersey. The brothers of Priscilla's Graham, Forney and Connor friends attended the Old North institution with Mecklenburg Polks, Iredell Osbornes, Cabarrus Phifers, and Rowan Chambers'. The Palmetto metropolis first attracted the Brevards who had South Carolina kin, and by the time Priscilla returned to Lincoln had educated also Unity Connors, Johnstons and Reids. Of the physicians, the University of Pennsylvania had a virtual monopoly.

"College keeps too many men from home," Priscilla complained. It was a condition lamented by all the socially minded contingent of her sex.

"It looks like every smart boy these days," her mother agreed, "thinks he has to be a lawyer, preacher or physician."

"Actually a small percentage of the total, my dear," Colonel Brevard remarked. "The majority of our youth of respectable connections are still taking land and Negroes for their portion instead of college."

Among the latter was Alec McIntosh of Hopewell. Recently home from General Graham's expedition against the Creek Indians in the war with England, Alec had chosen this Sunday to ride over from Mecklenburg for meeting at Unity.

Squire McIntosh, Alec's father, owned more slaves than

the Polks or Springs' and more land than the Alexanders.
In addition to these assets, Alec had the air of a Lothario
and the heart of Sir Galahad. Not even Lord Howard of
the Minstrel's lay sat a thoroughbred more easily than
he. Perversely, instead of selecting a chivalric name for
his dappled filly, Alec had elected to call her "Meg" after
Tam O'Shanter's plebeian nag.

"The girl can outrun the devil," he said, "and, like Tam,
that's what I need."

Priscilla observed the horse and rider with admiration.

"Do you think Alec McIntosh came to meeting to show
off his filly?" She directed her mother's attention to the
object of her own.

"I doubt it," her mother smiled. "The McIntoshes don't
have to do that. It's time he was looking for a wife."

The youngest Brevard daughter remarked enviously,
"I hear he can snap his whip for any girl in Mecklenburg."

"And this is Lincoln," Priscilla was immediately on the
defensive. The iron foundry heiresses were aware of their
increasing desirability. But Alec McIntosh wouldn't be
dazzled by warehouses full of dogirons and firebacks.

"Doubtless he only came for the service," said Mrs.
Brevard, sorry she had suggested any other motive. But
she did not believe what she said. Among the young men
who organized the French Deist Club and read heretical
books like Voltaire and Tom Paine were some of Alec's
closest cronies. He hadn't joined the club himself, probably
because it read too much, but he was congenial with its
members.

"He's improving the company he keeps," Priscilla
commented.

It would have shocked her no little had she known that one of these same infidels had suggested to Alec that the Brevard miss recently home from Charleston was worth a twenty mile canter to see.

During the sermon Priscilla found it difficult to keep her mind on Dr. McRee. Alec McIntosh was out of the class of the average up-country swain. Certainly he wouldn't be close with his money when he married and justify himself by John Calvin. And Alec had money coming. Unlike most Piedmont families the McIntoshes had not been prolific. Alec had no brothers or sisters.

"Probably he wouldn't expect a baby every other year," Priscilla concluded and suffered an unflattering heat for her impiety. But too many planters of her acquaintance had no interest beyond fertility of farm and family.

Priscilla remembered Alec's mother vaguely. A reputed heiress from up near Philadelphia, she had died some years ago. Even when past forty she had had a lovely graceful body, but her face had been pitted with small-pox scars. It was said she had had them from childhood, which may have explained her presence in the Carolina backwoods.

"I wonder if she wanted to live." Priscilla could conceive of no cross more onerous to bear.

Alec's wife wouldn't even have a mother-in-law. Not that Priscilla rejoiced unduly over Mrs. McIntosh's release from the flesh, but a man's mother in heaven was always a blessing to his wife below.

As a future, Priscilla's instincts counseled, Alec McIntosh was a man with an ideal past.

CHAPTER 3

CLOUD OVER CATAWBA

DURING THE INTERVAL between sermons, the unsuspecting cause of Alec's presence at Unity was busily planning maneuvers for abetting him.

"Pa," she said carelessly, "why don't you invite Alec McIntosh to eat with us? He came alone and I don't see any basket on his horse."

"If I could attribute that to Christian charity," her father smiled, "I'd do it." Like most men with attractive daughters he found his irresistible. "Don't you think an invitation would come with better grace from your brother, under the circumstances?"

Priscilla flushed at being so obviously exposed, but she saw that her father had made a point. The man at least should be given a chance to decline. Brother Joe had long known Alec and willingly took the initiative, but he saw little of his guest. A few passing comments on Joe's health and generosity and Alec was at Priscilla's side.

"La, Mr. McIntosh," she said, "I'm surprised to see you at meeting." She shouldn't have been. She had seen him often enough at Hopewell when she was younger. But evidently he was seeing her today for the first time. Mrs. Brevard considerately kept the younger sisters out of his view.

"Charleston has agreed with you," he observed. Priscilla had acquired a fetching poise. Her blonde hair, brown eyes, and chiselled features made her, as Alec had been warned, "a natural for looks." And her blue silk pelisse and satin bonnet trimmed with feathers were daring innovations for the time and place.

"It's an agreeable city," she answered, "but I'll take our hills for a permanent abode." Then patriotically from *The Last Minstrel*: "This is my own, my native land."

Alec recognized the quotation but decided against a dialogue on the poets.

"Only I do wish," Priscilla added, "that our people had more of the *joie de vivre*." Priscilla's French came not from the Brevards, who had long outlived it, but from the Mademoiselle at the Seminary.

"Lincoln County should have a St. Cecilia and a St. Andrews Society," she declared. "Alas, for Euterpe and Terpsichore on the Catawba!"

Although a gentleman's schooling did not include Jaudon's *Polite Learning*, Alec was acquainted with the Muses from the Reverend Caldwell's classical school. He grinned an agreement.

"Even Pa's Society of the Cincinnati never gives a ball here," Priscilla went on. "They do in Charleston and wear full regimentals. You Mecklenburgers have a ball room over the courthouse in Charlotte, don't you? But I shouldn't be talking about that at meeting."

"After Charleston," Alec commented, ignoring her caution, "you may find Charlotte a trifle one-horse, but it will grow. Salisbury claims twice our size and I guess has its points, but it smells like sausage and sauerkraut to me. I never could understand the Deutsch.

"What were the gay blades up to in Charleston?" he changed to a more congenial subject. "The last time I was there it was fancier than Philadelphia."

"The war," Priscilla sighed, "closed the Broad Street Theater. But the Washington Course was open and Vaux Hall Gardens has a new amphitheatre." She started to hum "Hail, Columbia" and remembered suddenly where she was.

"The Scotch Presbyterians have completed a beautiful church on Meeting and Tradd," she remarked loud enough to be overheard. "I attended service there usually. Though I did go to the Huguenot Church several times. Pa's people were Huguenots, you know. That is, until grandmother MacWhorter got hold of them. Since then we've been as Scotch as the Alexanders."

She didn't add "and as rich" but it was an old saw in Mecklenburg that the abundance of Alexanders accounted for the scarcity of Jews.

The congregation began reassembling for the afternoon sermon. Customarily this service at Communion was for the unprofessed or tokenless attendants, but Dr. McRee had invited all to remain. The Precentor was snapping his tuning fork as a signal for the opening hymn.

"I'm not staying," Alec announced. "It looks like a thunderstorm out here, and there's sure to be another inside. With your permission, I'd be glad to ride home with you. That is, if you're considering it."

Priscilla looked up at the sky.

"*Ma foi!*" she exclaimed. A French miss would have said "*mon dieu*" but Priscilla was, as she had admitted, mostly Scotch. "There's no one at home but Diana and Sappho," she remembered. "They're sure to sleep through anything. Maybe Ma would want me to take Cato and see about the house."

Ma was worried herself about leaving the windows open without specific instructions. All except the two house girls, who had been purchased recently and weren't communicants, were here for the observance.

"You'd better start now," she told Priscilla privately and without consulting her husband. Men had a way of imputing matrimonial motives to everything a woman did. "Mr. McIntosh won't expect to come in since there's no one at home."

Then she added in a more audible tone, "Be sure and have the shutters latched from the inside. The banging will break the panes if they are loose." Glass panes were a luxury few but quality like the Brevards thought needful.

The three set off immediately over the still dusty red road. The rabbit tobacco, bull nettle, and rag weed along the ditch were covered with a fine layer of rusty looking earth. Gathering clouds had cooled the air and atmospheric changes stirred it softly.

Priscilla had a new side-saddle for her palfrey and Cato stumped along on a piebald mule some distance behind. All Piedmont girls could ride but at Priscilla's touch, a Low-country gallant had told her, a horse took on the grace of a gazelle. As they passed each milestone, she swayed outward to read the numbers and show how secure she was in the stirrup.

Alec's filly was as coy and skittish as his companion. He was delighted by the whimsical, obvious archness of both. When he brushed a green fly from Meg's withers, he touched her as gently as he would have touched Priscilla

A couplet from his favorite, Bobby Burns, seemed very apropos:

A fine pacing horse, wi' a clear chained bridle
A whip by her side and a bonie side-saddle.

"Charming, Mr. McIntosh," Priscilla applauded. "But the first part of that, if you remember, was not so complimentary. The gentleman was tempting the lady with worldly goods."

Alec agreed that it was a wicked advantage. To himself he observed with satisfaction, "She's at least aware that they are a temptation."

By the time they arrived at Catawba Forge, Alec had obtained permission to call within the week, and, as a proper escort, bade "Miss Priscilla" goodbye at the gate.

Cato put up the mounts and Priscilla remembered, after appraising her effect in the pier-glass, to wake up the house girls and get the shutters latched. The late summer lightning had begun to flash. In the distant mountains, thunder rumbled threateningly.

Priscilla had forgotten how deathly afraid of lightning she was when alone. It suddenly occurred to her that alone she was. She couldn't permit Diana and Sappho to see that she was frightened, these were new Negroes and it was dangerous to relax too soon. They would have to stay out in the yard kitchen. Her nerves involuntarily tightened for the strain. Above, the clouds filtered the sun to a gleaming twilight.

A sudden clap of thunder announced that the storm had arrived. Priscilla had been unconsciously counting between each flash and its accompanying report. If she got as far as seven before the thunder, the lightning was a mile away. The last loud crack came right after the flash. She fled upstairs to the room she shared with her sisters. Always before one of them had been there to keep her company in the high bed.

Priscilla jumped onto the feather mattress, disdaining the leisurely mounting stairs. A second deafening report roared out. She could see the red light through the shutters.

It brightened the room like a rocket. She waited tensely after each explosion for the next. The crack of the lightning became almost as loud as the thunder. The floor of the heavy house shook and the precious panes rattled.

A new song, "The Star Spangled Banner," kept ringing in Priscilla's mind. "Rockets' red glare, bombs bursting in air." The climax of storm and song combined to unnerve her. From the grandeur of both she sensed only a thrill of terror.

She began to pray. "O Lord, I've had worldly thoughts ever since I got home. I promise to be better. Don't let me die in this house alone."

A bolt of flame struck a tree outside her window and the crash of branches, smell of fire and house-rocking roar made her jump out of bed. A large wardrobe stood across from the windows. She fled into it and pulled the doors together after her. Her teeth were chattering and her skin contracting with goose flesh. Not since she had been lost in the bamboo thicket at the age of five had she known such agony.

"Rockets' red glare, bombs bursting in air!"

Priscilla prayed aloud. "I promise not to think of fine houses anymore. I'll burn up the portrait if You want me to. I'll,—O Jesus, please, please, please." Crash followed on crash. Although the closed wardrobe seethed like the foundry forge, Priscilla pulled capes and robes over her head and buried herself on the floor.

The storm began to subside slowly. It took a long time to move on. When she cracked the doors a little to peer out a new flash darted through. To her fears were added the dread of another earthquake like that of four years before. The stifling heat of her hideout could presage anything. In complete exhaustion she finally slept.

Her mother found her on the closet floor when she returned with the family and servants after meeting.

"Nothing but electricity, Priscilla," Mrs. Brevard reminded her. "Your Jaudon explains it very clearly. At your age you should be ashamed to hide in a wardrobe." But having been brought up without *Polite Learning*, Mrs. Brevard reverted to an earlier recourse. "You must pray God to strengthen your faith. If your time has come, you can't hide from Him. If it has not, you have nothing to fear."

Priscilla had never understood Predestination with any comfort to her future. She did not doubt the omnipotence of Providence yet what was the good of prayer if it couldn't intervene? She was shamed by the betrayal of her weakness. Sixteen was maturity for a woman and she had friends already married with babies. In the safety of family and sunlight, she thought guiltily of her promises to the Lord.

"If He wanted me to burn the portrait," she reasoned, "He'd have given me a sign. I said 'If You want me to'. " The fine house presented other difficulties. "That will be my husband's business, anyway." She couldn't help what he might think.

Yet, unless he did some thinking on the subject, he wasn't very likely to be Priscilla Brevard's husband.

CHAPTER 4

CLOUD OVER CATAWBA

THE REVEREND PETER McCLELLAND had a small up-river church, over a hundred miles as the current ran, from his own and Priscilla's section of Lincoln County. For one session he had distinguished himself at Hampden-Sidney College in Virginia, then his savings went to release his father from imprisonment for debt. Unwilling to accept presbytery charity, he hired himself out in Steele Creek and completed his theology under the tutelage of Dr. Humphrey Hunter.

Ever since he could remember he had watched Priscilla sitting primly in the Brevard's hooded pew at Unity. The McClellands occupied a rear bench. To Peter she represented all the unobtainable ambitions of life on this earth. To his many brothers and sisters, none of whom had been advantaged further than a few months at the old field school, she was a priss and a prig.

A camp meeting in Lincoln County gave Peter McClelland an opportunity to visit Catawba Forge on a professional mission. The Brevards, of course, were hardly expected to attend, although there were two Presbyterian evangelists, counting Peter, and only four Methodists and Baptists. The object of his visit was a contribution of lumber for the construction of the ministers' stand.

Peter was met at the door by Sappho and shown into the parlour while the Negress searched for her master. As the Colonel was being fitted for a pair of pantaloons, Mrs. Brevard came in to greet their guest.

"I'm so glad you stopped, Peter," she gave him her

hand. "It does seem that you're farther from Unity at Goshen than you were in Virginia."

"Thank you, Ma'm," Peter replied, "I feel like it myself. But I'm preaching at home, you know, this week, at the camp ground."

"I hope we can get there," Mrs. Brevard lied pleasantly. "You've learned so much now though I doubt if we can follow you. We haven't seen anything at all of you since you got back." Hampden-Sidney was two years in the past but it seemed tactful to stress Peter's educational elevation. "Maybe you've got a lady-love in Steele Creek?" The equality shouldn't be pressed too far.

Peter reddened. "No, Ma'm. It was Dr. Hunter's books held me down."

"But we keep up with you from your brothers." This contained elements of truth. Mrs. Brevard rarely failed to ask Josiah McClelland, who served as overseer on a nearby plantation, how Peter was progressing, and she did see his brother Saul rather frequently, Saul being a mechanic who did odd repair jobs in the vicinity. But if she elicited information from Saul on any subject she did better than anyone else who wore shoes on weekdays.

Priscilla broke in at the front door, beating off the gnats with her riding crop. Before she observed whom her mother was entertaining she was inside the parlour.

Peter stood up by his chair. He was tall, well-knit and bronzed. In contrast to the darkening of his skin, the sun had whitened his tow head with striking effectiveness. Priscilla was startled by a slight shock of admiration.

"Why, Reverend McClelland," she managed to gasp, "I didn't know horses could pull you from Goshen."

"As a fact, Miss Priscilla," he replied, "they didn't. I

came down the River on a raft. We're holding a camp meeting in Lincoln and I'm asking your father for some sawed wood."

"I'm sure Pa'll be happy to give it to you," Priscilla said. The devil prompted her to add "You'll need some round poles for the folks who get the jerks" but she resisted the impulse and bit her tongue at her temerity. Her confusion colored her cheeks with a deceptive blush. Mrs. Brevard made a covering remark on riding in the heat. Before Priscilla had time to adjust her thinking to an appropriate sentiment on the revival, her father came in and she and her mother retired.

For a moment Peter was unable to respond to the greeting of his host. A hot flash of insensibility followed his bow to Priscilla. As she passed from the room her riding crop touched his leg and the seductive odor of clean perspiration raced the blood through his head. Fortunately Colonel Brevard mistook his hesitation for the not unusual ill ease of the poor in the parlours of the rich.

"We are honored, Peter," he attempted to free the young minister from constraint. "I hope your family is well."

"Very well, Sir," Peter recovered himself. "Thank you, Sir."

Colonel Brevard listened politely as Peter opened the object of his call. Back in the early years of the century, the Brevards and others in their circumstances had supported their clergymen to the extent of attending the first of the open air revivals. But the shouts and groans of the worshippers, which the preachers seemed rather to evoke than to repress, began by embarrassing and ended by alienating the conservative element. Other objections soon arose to strengthen their aversion.

Colonel Brevard permitted his guest to conclude his request uninterrupted. "With respect to the lumber, Peter," he began, "it is yours for whatever use you wish to make of it. If my silence with respect to the meetings is of any advantage to you, you may have that also. I cannot, however, promise you either my participation or my approval."

Peter's reaction was evident only from the slight moisture on his lip and forehead. His host continued.

"You will not, I am sure, object to my frankness as we are by now old friends. According to my interpretation of the fourth Commandment six days of labor are as obligatory as one of rest on the seventh. During camp meetings of any duration there is little work done. Crops suffer, and with respect to responsibility, character likewise. Many in your gatherings can ill afford the time. That you are persuaded of higher values, I know. I am ready to concede your convictions if you will honor me with the same consideration."

"No one, Sir," Peter rose to go, "would question your loyalty to the principles of our faith. I thank you for the lumber and will bring over a wagon, if agreeable, tomorrow."

"There's no need for that," said the Colonel extending his hand, "I will send it to the camp ground."

As Peter opened the iron gate from the yard, his eye was caught by the stray tassel of a riding crop. It lay at the base of the rock wall. Peter picked it up in closing the foot latch. For the four miles he walked from Catawba Forge to the small stone hut of his parents, he held it tightly in his hand.

Priscilla sat with her arms around her knees in a large wooden tub. Over her shell pink back Diana poured warm water from a pail. Two small ebony flashes formed a bucket brigade to the caldron in the kitchen yard.

"Dat Reveren'," queried Diana, "am he comin' courtin'?"

"Certainly not," replied Priscilla with more asperity than the question warranted.

"He a han'some man," Diana continued, "but Aun' Mauna say he ain't fittin' for the likes of us."

"Aunt Mauna shouldn't talk like that," Priscilla found herself defending the preacher. "Mr. McClelland went to college in Virginia. He's no buckra." But she couldn't forget his sisters, hoeing potatoes in their big sunbonnets and bare feet.

She had not been oblivious to the intent grey eyes on the back bench through all these years. Peter had been a serious little boy. He almost never laughed, but he never cried either. One Sunday during the interval, when the children were washing in the creek, Peter had preached them a sermon. In spite of the jeers of the older boys he had kept on till he finished and Priscilla had wondered why God didn't strike the scoffers dead.

Now that he was an ordained minister he could protect his wife from the wrath of God. He could get her into heaven no matter what guilty yearnings tormented her conscience. You'd have to be pious, though, because preachers' wives were always an example to the other women. And you couldn't dress up much, even if you took your own seamstress to the manse.

"Is you sleep, Miss 'Scilla?" asked Diana.

Priscilla laughed. "Not in this tight squeeze. Here, give me a drying cloth and let me stand up."

On top of her chest, Priscilla saw the drops and beads

which Uncle Joseph Brevard had brought up from Camden. When she got into her petticoats she faced the mirror and clipped the drops through her earlobes. Their pale blue radiance flattered the petal pink of her cheeks and neck. She turned her head approvingly. But her brothers would make fun of her if she wore them to supper with no one there except the family. Reluctantly, she replaced them in the box.

The wives of Presbyterian preachers rarely wore jewelry, only a little gold was permissible. She walked over to the window and looked at the sky. Not a cloud dimmed the heavens. What fool thoughts were taking up her time. Peter McClelland!

"I wonder what Alec McIntosh would think of these ear rings?" she mused. "I wonder what he thinks of me."

CHAPTER 5

CLOUD OVER CATAWBA

ALEC MCINTOSH did a good deal of thinking. He wanted a wife who would make him want to work. Until now the routine oversight of the lands and Negroes which had become his at twenty-one had been an obligation not without interest but lacking in inspiration. Accumulation for itself was pointless to Alec. Already McIntosh titles outnumbered those of Alexander in the Mecklenburg deed books. He lacked a focus for his creative energies.

Priscilla's physical and social perfections presented a challenge. Like a diamond in the Piedmont quartz, she deserved a more ornate setting than was as yet available in the Catawba Valley. To provide this setting stirred Alec's faculties to straining eagerness. As often as Meg was tied to the gate at Catawba Forge, and that was often enough to arouse all Unity's speculation, Alec's ambitions soared higher for the temple in which to house his goddess. No one should erect the shrine but himself, and none but he should worship in its inner sanctum.

In his cooler moments he admitted the extravagance of his idealization. That Priscilla longed to live as befitted her charms was as obvious as the charms themselves and detracted nothing from them for Alec. She would love the master of "Branksome's lordly hall" because its perfections to her must, of necessity, be a reflection of its builder.

The Reverend Peter McClelland gave Alec small concern. He knew him by sight only and felt for him the generous admiration he was ready to accord any man who rises by merit above the station into which he was born. That a woman of Priscilla's cultivation would volun-

tarily receive the addresses of a camp meeting revivalist
did not appear to him within the realm of credibility.
From some of his free-thinking friends there had been
pointed thrusts with respect to his soul-saving rival, for
the Reverend Mr. McClelland had called rather oftener at
Catawba Forge than his obligation for the lumber required. But Alec had attended one meeting, on the out-
skirts of the crowd and in the safety of Meg's saddle, and
came away convinced that the competition was slight.

His conviction was fundamentally correct. Whatever
the minister's future aspirations, his past had given him
insufficient confidence for surmounting in one hurdle
the forbidding wall between Unity Brevard and Unity
McClelland. Priscilla had been less woman than she was
to feel no elation in the young man's obvious discomposure
in her presence. To toy with her power by a parting of
the lips or an attentive protruding of a pink tongue was
beyond her control to resist. But life as the mistress of a
country manse formed no part of her fair-weather thinking.

So naively evident, indeed, was Priscilla's price that
Alec found subtlety a needless deviation from his goal.
There was a minimum requisite of public company-keep-
ing which must be observed for Presbyterian proprieties.
Mr. McIntosh and Miss Brevard were seen together at
Dickson's Old Field for the General Muster of the Lincoln
County militia. During Court Week in Lincolnton and
Charlotte, Alec acted in turn as guest and host of the
Brevards for the festivities. In conclusion, he sat with
Priscilla's brothers in their Unity pew and accepted their
hospitality for the interval meal.

These regulation irrelevancies attended to, Alec got

down to fundamentals on a Monday morning with a roll of architect's sketches.

"My father got some ideas from President Jefferson in Washington," he told Priscilla. "While Mr. Jefferson was in Europe he made a study of Greek and Roman buildings, and I think he has hit upon an appropriate adaptation for us in the South. I like his theory that our civilization here since built on slavery like that of the Athenians may logically develop like theirs."

Priscilla was better versed in the feudal lore of Scottish lairds and castle keeps but, as Alec pictured it, a Greek democracy had its possibilities.

"The Athenian aristocracy," he explained, "ruled for the good of Athens, and the Southern leaders have learned the same from Plutarch and Plato. I was even exposed to some of it myself in Parson Caldwell's school. If we adopt the standards of their statesmen we might as well take a lesson also from their architects.

"Now this house," Alec pulled a roll from his boot, "as sketched by Mr. Jefferson has a portico of four Ionic columns."

A little gasp of admiration escaped Priscilla. It was all she had ever dreamed. And she had been dreaming. Since her foreswearing in the storm she had consciously put mansions and manor houses out of her thoughts, but day and night dreams were beyond her control and castles in the air had continued to float through her mind.

The combination of the strength of Georgian brick with the grace of Grecian columns was well suited to the temper of the McIntoshes. Priscilla was right. A man's personality does show in the house he builds. Behind the cement-covered pillars, the high wall of the front was broken by a fan-like transom over the entrance and an iron balcony beneath the windows. The balcony was Alec's decoy.

"I'll see that it's wrought to the Queen's taste," he said. "How would you like a monogram in an iron heart? P.B. and M. form a natural consolidation."

For days Priscilla had carried her vinaigrette of fainting salts for just this moment. For weeks she had rehearsed "no" in English and in French to make it sound like "yes." Only women passed twenty said "yes" the first time. But Alec's peculiar temptation had completely seduced her. Her ecstasy precluded the feeblest form of protest.

"Oh, Alec," she sighed, "when can we start?"

The accepted suitor was a trifle disconcerted. He had envisioned a more personal plighting of the troth. But if there was a kiss in Priscilla it was for Thomas Jefferson. Alec's disappointed grimace flickered by without Priscilla's notice.

"As soon as it's legal," he laughed helplessly.

Priscilla could not be arrested by details. She turned eagerly to the second page. "Is this the first floor plan?"

"Yes, my love. And the central hall is twenty feet wide." A spacious hall was a patent of nobility. At its end a curved stairway spiraled to a similar passageway above. The design was intelligible even to Priscilla's unprofessional eye.

"Oh, how lovely," she ran a pink finger around the corkscrew curves.

"The plaster work in the parlour," Alec continued, "doesn't show up in this. But there's a ceiling medallion that will give your friends a crick in the neck."

"And a crystal chandelier?" Priscilla added hopefully. A transparent pendant with a hundred prisms dangled before her.

"That's not up to the architect," Alec said solemnly. "But a buss will buy it."

"I'll take it at the price," she replied, "and pay for it when delivered." Alec blew a kiss into the air and gave it a parting salute.

"Now across from these windows," Priscilla went on, "couldn't we have recesses in plaster to balance them? Set-in walls are elegant for tapestries and paintings."

To the rear of the parlour was a long, narrow room for dining with a porch exit to the outside kitchen.

"Walnut wainscoting," she considered, "is appropriate for a dining room. Or could we have mahogany?"

"Anything you choose," Alec agreed. "One of these rooms across the hall," he ventured, "could be our bedroom."

Priscilla ignored the familiarity. "What is this long room over the parlour?" She stretched out the second story diagrams and studied the dimensions of the large apartment.

"Oh, Alec, it's a ballroom!"

Instead of four bedrooms upstairs, which meant a siege of breeding to fill, there were only two. The side of the house above the parlour was thrown into a single house-width apartment. For mantel and panelling, Alec had indicated marbleized wood. There wouldn't be a finer private ballroom in the State.

"No Irish jigs for this room," thought Priscilla. She envisioned only formal cotillions and stately minuets.

For the second-story bed chambers there would be flowered wallpaper and Alec let fall that it was already ordered from DuFour in France. There weren't half a dozen houses in the Piedmont with paper and none, Priscilla was sure, with paper from France.

"All the outbuildings," Alec explained, "are to be brick. The kitchen, the well, the carriage, soap and smoke houses are sketched on this sheet to conform to the central building. We might even build the darkies' houses of brick. I've seen some in South Carolina."

Priscilla hadn't reached the yard in her planning. She was busy furnishing the interior of the house. She would have a grandfather clock, of course, like the one the Burton's got from Boston and she wouldn't have to cut a hole in her ceiling to stand it up. Of course, Alfred Burton had plans for a big house later but not so grand as Alec's.

Like the Burtons, too, she would have silver forks. The two-tined steel implements generally in use were hardly respectable. She had seen at Bondo's and at Reynal's in Charleston as beautiful silver as could be bought in America. She could go down with Alec and pick it out. When he went North he could bring back a Duncan Phyfe dining room suite and ask in Philadelphia if any of the famous Stiegal glass his mother owned was still for sale.

"Do you know, Alec," she said, "we can get almost everything we need in this country? Ma said your mother told her that most of the nice things they used to have in Pennsylvania had to be ordered from England. There'll be master craftsmen in Charlotte by the time our children grow up."

"I'm glad you're looking out for them," Alec laughed, "but aren't you travelling a trifle fast? You haven't even seen where the house is going to be."

Priscilla thought a moment. "It's nearly twelve now and dinner must be ready. Ma's had a place set for you, of course. After we eat you could speak to Pa and then it would be all right for me to ride over the River with you this afternoon."

Her innocent efficacy was acknowledged by Alec's grin. "If all your planning is as much to my benefit, Mrs. McIntosh," he agreed, "I'll promise to 'obey' when we're married."

Priscilla blushed at the implied reflection. "I'm sorry, Alec. Oh, I am a vain and headstrong person and I know God will punish me for it. You'll help me, won't you?"

"I'll need help myself if I ever have to call you down," he smiled. "Except, I believe, on one minor oversight. For that, maybe, experience will provide a cure." He took a quick survey of the garden where they sat and a longer one of Priscilla's contrite brown eyes.

"Don't people usually kiss to seal a marriage pact?" And without waiting for a reply he pressed his mouth on Priscilla's parted lips.

The loud clang of the plantation bell interrupted his searching.

"La, Mr. McIntosh, you wouldn't let a bell scare you?" Priscilla pretended a sophistication she did not possess. But as Alec was twenty-six he was neither fooled nor disappointed. A goddess had to be taught the ways of the world. And he felt like a teaching god.

After dinner Colonel Brevard was not surprised to be asked for a word in private by his guest. Gentlemen didn't call in the mornings without declarative intentions. Nor was Alec greatly surprised when the Colonel suggested that instead of giving Priscilla land and slaves her father would like to take him into the iron business.

"You won't have a great deal to do," the Colonel told him. "And there's no necessity for removing to this locality, but I'd like to feel that my life's work is of interest to my son-in-law. It was my father-in-law who set up the foundry." Since almost all of the kitchen utensils and farm implements of the Piedmont were made in Lincoln County, Alec was not averse to accepting a share in so lucrative a trade. The Brevards, Grahams, Fullenwiders and Forneys had more ready cash than many who owned double their land.

Alec thanked the Colonel. "I'd like to build on the Catawba burying-ground tract father gave me in Mecklenburg. It's not far from the shoals, you know, and we can easily get back and forth." The Colonel knew the land and approved the selection.

"And if you've no objection, Sir," Alec continued, "I'll take Priscilla over this afternoon to see it." The Colonel had none whatever and forgot even to ask if they would try to come back by night.

Each had now exhausted all subjects which did not infringe on the privacy and prerogatives of the other, and Priscilla found them pulling furiously on their pipes in an unrelaxed silence.

The horses were in good spirits and trotted or cantered briskly without urging. It was more difficult to bring them to a walk on the downward grades. But as all four thoroughbreds were sure of themselves and of the favors of fortune to those who set the pace, they arrived with no casualty beyond a light film of red dust.

Alec had selected a green hill a hundred yards from the River. Without divulging his purpose, he suggested that they leave the road and ride to the top. All underbrush except the Judas trees and dogwood now in bloom had been cleared away. The pines left a mattress that silenced the hoof treds and gave the woods a sense of seclusion.

"You don't have to tell me, Mr. McIntosh, this is where I am going to live!"

The prospect from the hill top in every way suited the pretensions of an elegant establishment. Great black oaks, walnuts, and poplars shaded the summit. On three sides the slopes were covered by pine forests. That to the River, which was unseen from the road, had been cleared and sown in pea vines. The green vista to the coiling red Catawba filled Priscilla with elation.

"Down in the Low-country everything is flat," she said. "There's a thrill in looking over the rice fields from Governor Middleton's place but it could never be home. No wonder the rich people there have *ennui*. They have no variety."

Alec wanted her to go on. He loved his hills and loved her for loving them. But she was busy thinking. After a silence he spoke.

"The Catawba is our blood. In drought it's like a vein, in freshets like an artery. Someday we may dig it out and float our cotton to Charleston. Or maybe the falls can be used for more power than mill wheels and we'll develop something new in the world. Whatever comes to the Piedmont, the Catawba's going to play a big part."

"Alec, what'll we name our house?" Priscilla was weighing the merits of "Catawba Crest" and "McIntosh Hall." "Which do you prefer?"

"Something more personal," Alec grinned.

"I like 'Belmont'," Priscilla went on, "but the Osbornes in Iredell have had that so long it belongs to them. There are too many Mounts, Groves, and Woods already. We ought to be original."

"We shall," Alec said.

"You've already got a name for it, Alec McIntosh, and you're afraid to tell me. I promise to like it if you do."

"Priscilla's Price." And he kissed her as he would have kissed a pretty child.

CHAPTER 6

CLOUD OVER CATAWBA

THE PUBLICATION of the banns for the approaching marriage of Alexander McIntosh and Priscilla Brevard met with the approval of Unity's elect. A hundred miles upriver, the Reverend Peter McClelland read and reread a half literate letter from his sister.

deer brother—yoor prowd gal is goin to marrie the rich one from Meklinburg—for mysel I think yoor well shut of her—she is prettie alrite but wud want for more than yoor goin to git with colidge and everything—folks say its ter be a big come off—I rekon you will be bid but if you think well of yoorsel you will sta home like us. Ma is been poorly and Sue is still got them sores in her eyes—doctor Macleen come out but we air thru with him fer not takin the hen—he said—save yer chikens and I will git yer fee out of the Graams and the Bravorts—he can save his visits here

Yoor sister until death
Melissa Anne McClelland

Peter sat staring at the quills and sand box on his bare pine table. His clenched fists banged against the rungs on his chair. Try as he would he could not rid his mind of Priscilla as his own. The pen in his hand would write only her name and "McClelland." Suddenly, with an expletive much like the "Damn!" of a layman he ceased to struggle and let the hot waves roll over him.

Priscilla clad in a low-cut gown danced a minuet across his table. In the scanty attire of a Richmond actress she offered him a glass of wine. Covered only by a night rail which clung to her form like wet hair on a bitch she lighted a candle and walked slowly toward his bedroom.

Peter stretched himself upon the floor and heaved with dry sobs. As the intensity of his passion spent itself, he rose to his knees and pulled the chair to him. With hands clasped until the sweat rolled from every finger crevice, he besought his Maker for forgiveness and strength.

But I say unto you, That whosoever looketh on a woman to lust after her, hath committed adultery with her already in his heart.

His prayer was interrupted by a knock at the door. In a thick voice, Peter called "Come in." One of his elders entered the room, gave the young minister a questioning look and sat down. Instead of speaking he stared hard at Peter's face. The preacher could find no words and the silence lasted for several minutes.

The old man rose. "My son," he said, "we are all young once. I cannot condemn you for sins I know too well. But remember the Proverb of Solomon 'Look not thou upon the wine when it is red.' My business can wait."

Peter sprang forward to stop him. "I am not drunk, Mr. Watson. You must believe me." He blew his breath in the old man's face. "I am not well but I have had no liquor. I'll be all right. Come back tonight."

But if Mr. Watson, or anyone else, came that night to the log cabin in which Peter lived he did not find the minister at home. Peter and his raft were floating past the haw, persimmon and bamboo of the Catawba banks. The moon was out but the current was too swift for a leisurely voyage. Peter worked hard to pole the makeshift craft

around the rocks and over the rapids. He had little energy
left for thinking.

When he reached the cove near his father's home, night
had again fallen. He tied up the raft and walked rapidly
in the direction of Catawba Forge. In spite of the constant
tugging and jolting on the River he felt an exhilaration
with each step closer to Priscilla. The four miles were
accomplished in little more than half an hour.

In sight of the flickering lights of the big house, Peter
stopped short. Why had he come? What possible ease
to the ache in his heart could the sight of Priscilla provide?
He stood foolishly still and looked about him. A bright
object at his feet arrested his attention. It was an ear drop.
Could it be hers? As he held it close to his face an escap-
ing perfume quickened his senses. Too often had the same
sensation suffused him in the presence of Priscilla.

He would keep it always. This much, at least, of Priscilla would be his to have and to hold. A bitter laugh
cut his thoughts. A gift from Mr. McIntosh, no doubt?
Probably worth a lot of money. He would return it, return
it tonight and see Priscilla. He would see her alone. He
would hold her arms and talk in her face. Never before
had he mustered courage to declare himself. Perhaps she
loved him? A Brevard woman would conceal such a
secret until she died, unless he spoke. He would speak
tonight. The way she let down her eyes the last time he
said goodbye. There was something to that. Not in a girl
of his class, they were bold because they had to be. But
a quality girl would never betray herself. What a fool he
had been!

Within fifty yards of the house he stopped again.

Voices floated out from the piazza, an unfamiliar male voice and Priscilla's.

"Do you think they'll ever go to bed?" It was Mr. McIntosh, Peter was sure.

"Not until you leave," Priscilla spoke very low and laughed in a way she had never laughed with him. "This isn't New England, you know."

"Gad!" said Alec stretching. "I wish it were. The Saints of Boston for all their piety knew more about comfortable courting than the Presbyterians will ever learn."

"You're holding my hand, aren't you?"

"This little fluff?" Alec kissed the palm. "If I squeeze it, it'll disappear."

"You aren't supposed to squeeze until you're married. Mr. McTarvish squeezed his girl so hard he broke her rib the night before the wedding. Everybody in Unity was laughing about it."

"I'll stand up to the ridicule if you'll let me try."

Peter McClelland felt heavy and tired. He wondered if his feet would carry him to his father's house. Turning toward the road he stepped recklessly on a pile of dry twigs.

"What was that?" said Priscilla.

"A chipmunk, perhaps," Alec laughed, "or maybe a squirrel. Whatever it was, you'll never know. Have you ever thought of all the mysterious things that go on around us? A change in the course of a river or a life may come from a rolling stone or a broken stick."

"You talk like a philosopher."

"And feel like a lover. I'm hiding it to save my face.

Here, by the way," he reached into his pocket, "is something that can be saved by yours."

Peter saw the gleam of a jewel as Priscilla put the drop in her ear.

"They're beautiful!" Priscilla caressed them with her voice. "Mr. McIntosh, you stole my blue one to give me these!"

"No, I swear I didn't. Did you lose one? I'll get you another. What was it like?"

"You know Pa won't let me take jewelry. That is, not until we're married. Keep these a little while for me, but bring them in your pocket when you come tomorrow."

So the earring Peter had found was not a lover's gift. Then he would not return it. It was hers before she belonged to someone else. It was Priscilla undefiled. She would forget it as she had forgotten him. Mrs. Alexander McIntosh would have plenty more, more than she could wear if she lived in Charleston.

He turned again to go. To see Priscilla in the arms of another man sickened him like sin. More than one twig snapped and more than one branch closed with a swish behind him in his blind retreat.

Priscilla was no longer aware of the outer world. Her thoughts had progressed from ear drops to chandeliers, from chandeliers to ballrooms, and from ballrooms to mansions exceeding anything the Catawba Valley had ever seen.

CHAPTER 7

CLOUD OVER CATAWBA

"WHILE THE RITE of matrimony is not a sacrament," Elder Knox had said, "holy wedlock is ordained by the Scriptures. Undue levity is unbecoming."

It was a long hail from the colonial Piedmont when the Reverend Alexander Craighead had ladled out a piquant nuptial punch. Since the turn of the century and the beginnings of the camp meetings, the pious frowned more and more on marriage festivities. They had almost eliminated the fiddle and the jig. Weddings were in danger of becoming as solemn as wakes.

To Colonel Brevard the hysterical revivals had fostered a "religious distemper" and he was resolved to give his eldest daughter an infare consonant with her position in the community. Long before the Colonel's decision respecting the hospitality of his house, the hope-chests of the distaff Brevards were replete with equally un-Calvinistic innovations.

"I know it's tempting fate," Priscilla admitted, "to buy your veil before you find the man to take it off. But everybody in Charleston was buying Brussels lace to lay by for something." Nothing like Priscilla's had been seen in Lincoln County. Bordered with orange blossoms and centered with arrow-pierced hearts, it was a wedding or pure waste. Yet barring the smallpox, Priscilla had little to fear from spinsterhood and knew it.

"Sensible forethought," observed Mrs. Brevard, "is not tempting fate but is rather an aid to fortune. When you girls began to grow up I had your father bring home a bolt of India muslin from Philadelphia. This is our first occasion for cutting it."

Priscilla was emboldened to further confessions. "The Mademoiselle showed us some descriptions of wedding gowns in *La Belle Assemblée*. She let me keep the page,— just in case."

"And I," said Mrs. Brevard, "believe I clipped a few of the same from the *Ladies' Museum*. Just in case."

Her daughters became hilarious over the revelations. Who would have thought that wedding bees still buzzed in Ma's bonnet! With two colored seamstresses, the girls and their mother spent a gay hour selecting a becoming cut. The Grecian drape was now all the fashion. Its filmy, clinging folds must enhance but not immodestly reveal Priscilla's charms.

"Madam Jerome Bonaparte," remarked Mrs. Brevard, "was married in India muslin."

"Why, Ma!" the girls chorused, "we didn't know you kept up with the *beau monde!*"

"And a gentleman present," their mother continued without changing her voice, "declared he could put the whole thing in his pocket."

A wedding sure did things to Ma!

"But my daughters will wear plenty of petticoats," she concluded, back in character.

To grace properly a ceremony of elegance and fashion, Priscilla had set her heart on a genteel preacher.

"We mustn't offend our own," her mother interposed.

"It's Priscilla's wedding, my dear," the Colonel observed, "and I trust her only one. A prayer from Unity should be

sufficient. Alec McIntosh can afford two officiating clergymen. Whom would you like to have, daughter?"

"I'll bet Peter McClelland would be glad to marry her,"
a sister volunteered.

Neither Priscilla nor her mother found this amusing.
For several months their obscure caller had scarcely crossed
Priscilla's mind, although she had heard he was once
in the neighborhood. It was odd he had not stopped to
wish her well. Or was she presuming a flame she had not
kindled? Well, it wasn't important anyway.

"Only one preacher on the River is really *comme il faut*,"
she stated, ignoring her sister, "and that is Dr. McRee."

At her request, Alec secured the promise of the Center
pastor's services. Dr. McRee would be as lenient with respect to ceremony as public opinion permitted and sometimes even more so. If Priscilla had wanted an Anglican
bishop, Alec would have fetched one.

In Unity, Hopewell and Center congregations there was
much refurbishing of silk, bombazine and cambric dresses.
The materials being generally of sober colors did duty,
even amongst the well-to-do, for divers occasions. Piedmont matrons made little effort to ape the changing fash-
ions of the coast.

"Brocaded satins and Chinese embroidery," opined the
Forney girls' governess, "will never mix with Catawba
mud." But some of the emancipated misses from boarding
schools had brought them home to try.

The men had fewer problems. All sported broadcloth
coats, fancy waistcoats, stocks and high collars for dress
events. Boots with the close fitting pantaloons were acceptable in the up-country. The younger men were relieved

that the use of wigs was now confined largely to Revolutionary veterans.

"I trust," Colonel Brevard told his prospective son-in-law, "that you have no objection to a little elaboration of the customary infare?"

"On the contrary, Sir," Alec rejoined, "I was afraid the objections might come from you. Priscilla and I have already ten attendants to stand up with us."

"You can hardly do less," the Colonel said, "considering the relatives who expect you for the rounds. General George Graham, I understand, plans to honor you with a ball in the Charlotte courthouse. Priscilla will be yours then and you will decide on the propriety of it."

"We've already accepted," Alec laughed. They had agreed, in fact, to quite a Hymenelia amongst Priscilla's kin. The Osbornes of Belmont had a second story ballroom and the modish Mistress Margret was admittedly the queen of fashion in the western wilds. The Alexanders of Alexandriana lived in affluent country squiredom but the Brevards of Mount Tirzah entertained with a good deal of éclat. No one made merrier over a "splicing" than General Joseph Graham of Vesuvius Furnace. And at Rural Hill there were grandchildren galore and few objections to a frolic.

"For my own part," said Alec, "since I have no relatives, I think a two weeks' resort to Catawba Springs may be a fitting finale for the tour. I have a letter from the Proprietor."

"Captain John Reid," observed Colonel Brevard, "can be relied upon. He is an honest man."

"And a capital salesman," Alec agreed. "This is what he says: 'I assure you, my dear sir, that the sulphur, iron and magnesia of our seven springs will banish from you both any lingering vapors that may remain from your extensive celebrations.' "

And extensive they were.

It would be too much to say that none of the well-laid plans "gang a-gley." Unqualified approval could hardly be expected for an infare so much in excess of established precedents. Several of the ministers remained no longer than courtesy required, but none declined except the Reverend Peter McClelland. Living so far upriver, he caused no comment by his absence.

More than one of the Scotch elders looked askance at the Brevard prodigality. A black-eyed patriarch took occasion to quote *Haec Fabula Docet* with a longer finger at Priscilla, which set her in tears of vexation.

"It's a curse," she told Alec, "he's pronounced a curse upon us." When she said her prayers at night she included a petition for removal of the malediction. Not until the diversions of Charlottetown, Belmont, Vesuvius Furnace, and Rural Hill were things of the past was the illusion entirely dispelled.

"She had to cry about something, I guess," Alec consoled himself. "I'd rather have it that than getting used to me."

When the two were finally settled in a small brick cottage on burying-ground hill, the blissful plans for building relegated Priscilla's anxiety to her limbo of storms, small-pox and virginity.

Alec had had the brick cottage built as a future gate-house and office for the proposed mansion. Here he and Priscilla lived for half a year while an army of McIntosh slaves erected the exotic Catawba temple. Every nigger-head rock in the basement, every brick in the Flemish bond walls, every heart-pine shingle for the roof was laid under his watchful eye.

"John Stigerwalt," he told Priscilla, "is the best builder in the Piedmont. He will supervise the work and make any changes you like as we go along."

With Owen Biddle's *Young Carpenter's Assistant* opened to stairways and mantels, Alec, Priscilla and Mr. Stigerwalt searched for designs appropriate to the finest seat on the River.

Although Alec spoke in jest in dubbing his dwelling Priscilla's Price, the good citizens of western Carolina adopted the name in malicious earnest. It wasn't necessary that anyone have overheard Priscilla's revealing resolution to the portraitist. Everyone believed she married the house anyway.

But from the bias of their pious parsimony, Priscilla's acquaintances misjudged her fundamentally. Circumstances had altered her present estate but they could not reach back into her past. Few souls could pass unscathed through an adolescence purged by Calvinistic brimstone. Her earliest recollections were shadowed by the withering sarcasms of Reverend Humphrey Hunter for the pleasures of the flesh. She had cringed beneath the fiery eloquence of James Wallis of Providence and the more terrifying pathos of Samuel Caldwell of Sugaw Creek. By the standards of her critics, Priscilla was a better Presbyterian than they knew.

"Alec," she asked, "do you believe in Predestination?"

He thought a moment. "If it means," he replied, "that our actions are largely determined by a past over which we have no control, I guess I do."

"Well, I'd have to ask Dr. McRee. That sounds something like what he said. Pa and Ma have always believed in it and Pa has done all right. I don't think we ought to take any chances just when we're beginning." She hesitated a moment. "You used to associate with skeptics, Alec, and people talked about you. How could you go with those men and lead such a Christian life?"

"Oh, I was very skeptical of them, too," Alec assured her. "That club's been dead for years now."

Since her husband's conduct was in accord with Christian morality, Priscilla convinced herself that his convictions must of necessity be orthodox. Retribution, she believed, was sure to follow infidelity. They had too much to lose to be flirting with heresies. A preacher husband would have brought more confidence,—but that was about all.

Like other Predestinarians, Priscilla did not claim that her destiny here or hereafter was dependent upon her will. But like others also, her actions belied her profession. Salvation through works was a doctrine denied in creed, but honored, at least by the women, in observance. Priscilla's soul was often troubled in private to ascertain her place among the elect.

The morality of slavery had been little agitated in the Piedmont. A few of the Methodists and Baptists gave lip service to manumission, but few owned any Negroes to liberate.

"If we give the Negroes Christianity," Priscilla asked Alec, "how can it be wrong to own them?"

"Slavery," Alec retorted, "is an institution well buttressed by the Bible. Presbyterian ministers wouldn't own them otherwise." Since many of her acquaintance did, Priscilla's qualms on that score were easily laid.

With his wife as she was, Alec was entirely satisfied. Women needed religion to make matrimony endurable to them. He had no more wish to alter her faith than he did her physical perfections, and he made no attempt to convert her to his convictions.

The first six months on the Catawba's ancient hilltop were too full of delirious activity for misgivings on salvation. Priscilla's days were a flitting from one delight to another and her nights were filled with honey. How Alec acquired his adroitness in the intimacies of sex it was not for Priscilla to inquire. According to boarding school confidences, most husbands would be beasts in bed. Priscilla was gratified to discover that hers was as sensitive to her responses as when dancing a minuet.

"Mr. McIntosh," she told her friends, "is adequate for any situation. And he is never *de trop.*"

In consequence of her appreciation, Alec's ego was healthily inflated and his delight in her constantly renewed. Priscilla was sometimes stirred by a threatening sense of surrender. There were even times when she would rather look at Alec than the house. After which—it was funny how much he knew—he was spontaneously inspired to change a marbleized mantel to the genuine stone or a pewter wall-light to Waterford glass.

CHAPTER 8

CLOUD OVER CATAWBA

AT LONG LAST Priscilla's Price stood materially apparent to the community. The curious had not been encouraged to pry during the process of construction.

"Our house-warming," Priscilla told her husband, "will mark a new era on the River."

"I hope so," Alec answered. "Isolated splendor can get pretty chilly." Which sounded like just more philosophy to Priscilla.

With the last load of Thomas Elfe furniture, Reynal silver and a complete service of French china from Charleston came Polly Hayne, Eliza Hampton and Anne Rutledge. These were schoolmates who represented to Priscilla the gracious ways of the quality of the coast.

"I want them to see," she confided to Alec, "that not all the Catawba Valley is 'back-country'."

Opportunely, there would be services at Hopewell the Sunday before Priscilla's reception. The pulpit was vacant, but the Reverend Samuel Caldwell of Sugaw Creek had consented to give his former congregation a sermon.

"Of all ministers," Priscilla complained, "it had to be he." It was well known that Mr. Caldwell's camp meeting fervor was responsible for the breach between him and conservative Hopewell.

"But without Sunday meeting," she concluded, "we'd never get the invitations distributed." Any preaching was better than none. Priscilla looked forward to a becoming deference for the mistress of Mecklenburg's most elegant establishment.

Bright clothes, she well knew, would make the girls conspicuous at church, but Alec agreed with her that Hopewell's Rome was hardly in a position to demand conformity of St. Michael's Athens. Nothing was said on the point and the guests dressed in the taste to which they were accustomed.

The McIntosh carriage-party caused something of a flurry inside the rock-walled churchyard. A few of the older members tightened a little the straight lines of their lips, but the young were frankly delighted by the distinction conferred upon their congregation. Priscilla introduced her guests indiscriminately and was determined to brave it out with the most austere of the elders.

"They may as well get used to it," she nerved herself. "The same water flows in the Catawba as in the Santee."

What Hopewell thought was less important, for the moment, than the impression on her company. It was too bad the church had no spire. The membership was the wealthiest in the Valley and should have shed its pioneer bark. Over-hanging eaves on three sides of the frame building gave it a peculiar barn-like appearance. The new Scotch church on Meeting Street had twin towers and a Doric portico, yet its people professed the same Calvinism as Mecklenburg. She remembered the becoming Sunday bonnets she had admired while Dr. Leland preached. Aside from those of her guests, there were not two in Hopewell which differed in shape and color from the rest. All this would change under the influence of the way of life on McIntosh hill.

Priscilla made mental note of the families she counted on especially to give tone to her entertainment. Alec had insisted that all their acquaintances be included, the old and infirm for the afternoon and the gayer spirits for the evening. She intended to comply, but if any were overlooked it would not be those who occupied the higher tiers of Hopewell pews.

The Rosedale Alexanders were the least provincial and most socially elect of that numerous tribe. Dr. Joe was Princeton bred, impeccably tailored and dignified in demeanor. Being a free-thinker in religion, he might not be at church, but Priscilla was sure to see some of his family.

The Lattas of Latta Place were acceptable. Old Mr. James was a crank, but very rich and his daughters all went to Salem. The girls were a credit to any community, if only their father wouldn't talk about his money, and their mother, a Knox from Unity, about her soul.

The Hugh Torrances from Cedar Grove were, like the Lattas, comparative newcomers to Mecklenburg with no Revolutionary officers to give them prestige. But like the Lattas also they had made up for any deficiency in pedigree by amassing an immediate and respectable patrimony.

Any of the Wilson cousins would be an addition. Claiming relationship with British nobility, the Wilsons went in for blooded horses, dancing frolics and generous grog. But they were the kindest people in the County and dispersed a bountiful hospitality. If any citizens of Mecklenburg spoke the language of the world, they did.

Priscilla's maternal kin at Rural Hill and Holly-wood were even better fixed than the Torrances and the Lattas. Both plantations had superior mansion-houses for the River and Priscilla entertained hopes of invitations for her guests in return for her house-warming. There was bounty and to spare at both.

She would send a note by one of the servants to the
family of Captain John Springs. Next to the McIntoshes,
the Springs' owned more slaves than any planters in
Mecklenburg and the Captain's sons were amongst the
earliest students at the University at Chapel Hill.

Having accomplished her purposes with all but the last,
Priscilla found that other invitations and introductions
would have to wait for the interval between sermons. The
congregation was moving into the church and the family
had made enough of a stir already without coming in late
to its pew.

As she passed across the stone threshold, Priscilla heard
an old lady remark audibly, "The McIntoshes must think
mighty well of themselves to build a house like that."

Throughout the strains of "Old Hundred," Priscilla kept
wondering who the ancient gossip had been. "What a
presumptuous thing to say," she thought. "You don't
have to be proud to live differently from your neighbors.
Or do you?"

The Reverend Mr. Caldwell was reading his text for the
morning sermon, Proverbs the 16th chapter, the 18th
verse:

"Pride goeth before destruction, and an haughty spirit
before a fall."

Priscilla gave a start. She felt that all eyes were upon
her. But the preacher couldn't have done this intentionally.
How could he have learned over in Sugaw Creek that the
McIntosh house was completed this week? Not until she
had invited him for the afternoon party a quarter of an
hour past could he have known the significance of the day
to her. Preachers couldn't change their texts in fifteen
minutes. And he had accepted without hesitation.

What kind of fall was in store for the haughty? If Mr. Caldwell had wanted an appropriate text he should have chosen Matthew 7:25:

"And the rain descended, and the floods came, and the winds blew, and beat upon that house, and it fell not; for it was founded on a rock."

The McIntosh fortunes were as secure as the foundations of their house. How could it fall? There were nearly a hundred slaves, the best worth a thousand dollars apiece. Alec's share in the foundry would bring as much again as his cotton and grain. In addition, he had Pennsylvania bank stock left by his mother. And good real estate in the village of Charlotte which was bound to grow. If any young man in the Piedmont was well established, it was Alec McIntosh.

"Pride goeth before destruction, and an haughty spirit before a fall."

Priscilla's defenses crumbled before Mr. Caldwell's onslaught. Logic was pitifully inadequate to hold the floodgates of fear. It was all Priscilla could do to restrain tears of humiliation. Her day of triumph was turned to gall.

At the interval she pleaded a headache and left the remaining invitations to Alec. The Charlestonians, having no conception of the identification of fine houses with proud spirits, accepted Priscilla's excuse in good faith. But Alec wasn't fooled.

"Couldn't we leave before the second sermon?" Priscilla begged. Alec thought not. It would be an admission of guilt before the congregation and he would recognize none.

"If a horse throws you, Priscilla, what do you do?"

"Get on again, of course, Alec. Why are you asking me that?" But she knew well enough and sat through the succeeding two hours with prayers in her heart for humility.

After preaching was over, the Lattas insisted that Alec and Priscilla bring their guests down to Latta Place for refreshments. It suited all members of both parties. The Latta girls were home from Salem and longed for company. Mr. Latta had a new shipment of merchandise from Philadelphia and while no sale could be transacted on the Sabbath there was no harm in opening the pack for a look. Mrs. Latta wanted to know what news Priscilla had from Unity, and Priscilla was desperately anxious to get away from the church.

The white frame house nestled in a bend of the River two miles west of Hopewell. It had no porch and the entrance was on the end, which made the Charlestonians feel at home.

"I want to show you Mr. Latta's inside window," Alec told his guests. "He cut it from the hall to the parlour so he could look in from the stairs. Evidently the old man believes that 'a peep in time saves mesalliances'. "

The girls were vastly amused. "The Misses Latta," Alec continued "will marry well or not at all."

Priscilla fidgeted with irritation. "I wonder why Alec must talk about marriages for convenience," she thought. She had little to contribute to the persiflage.

A houseboy brought cold milk and cider from the wellhouse and Mrs. Latta served real Bohea tea instead of the customary dittany or sassafras. There were half a dozen pewter platters filled with gingerbread, tarts and sweetmeats.

"Thank heaven," Priscilla sighed, "there's no Johnny-cake." The sadiron standby was not unknown to respectable Hopewell society.

After refreshments, Betsy, Polly and Nancy Latta gathered about a little spinet and sang the Moravian hymns they had learned at Salem. The Low-country guests declared themselves enchanted.

"Your view of the River is charming," commented Anne Rutledge.

"And the Catawba," exclaimed Polly Hayne, *"quelle bonne surprise!* I once memorized Monsieur Freneau's poem 'On Arriving in South Carolina' which has a verse something like this

> There Congaree his torrent pours
> Saluda, through the forest roars
> And black Catawba laves his shores
> With waters from afar.

"I think the poet was color blind."

"It may look like red mud to visitors," Alec agreed, "but we who live on it know that it's Indians' blood."

"Vraiment, Mr. McIntosh, you're romantic," Eliza Hampton told him.

"Not all the time," Alec grinned. "If we don't get home pretty soon, there'll be Scotch blood shed by Ethiopians As you already know, our slaves own us, and I heard Priscilla tell her kitchen Sheba that we'd be back before candle-light."

CHAPTER 9

SUNDAY NIGHT SUPPERS were always cold, for no sweat work was required of the Negroes on the Sabbath. Customarily basket lunch was taken for the interval between sermons, but the girls had arisen late for breakfast and Priscilla had omitted this country touch. Mrs. Latta's tea served to tide them over.

After supper, which consisted chiefly of cold ham, chicken, lamb and pickled Catawba trout, as many of the servants as wished came to the big house for prayers. On many plantations the attendance of all hands was required, but Alec insisted that this not be compulsory. Most of the blacks came willingly. They liked to sing.

Uncle Jup acted as precentor. With a tuning fork of his own he set the key and from memory parcelled the lines as precisely as any white dignitary at Unity or Hopewell. The rhythmic voices of the Africans blended with mournful solemnity in the tunes of Windham, Dundee and Old Hundred. When the hymns were done, the Negroes sang spirituals of their own. This was a concession on the part of the McIntoshes. Many Presbyterians looked on these swinging chants as pagan.

To Priscilla the harmony brought the first peace she had known since morning. Conveniently, her city-bred guests found it equally soothing and on Alec's suggestion all retired early to conserve their energies for the morrow's festivities.

In their downy Elfe four-poster, Priscilla's pent emotions temporarily relaxed under Alec's caress. He asked no more than her responses indicated and soon her searching for security of spirit was sublimated in an effortless following of his lead. Alex hoped mightily that all her misgivings of conscience might be as easily resolved in ecstasy. At eighteen she should be pliant enough for moulding. If he could protect her from her past he had no fear for her future.

No one arose except Alec until long after the sun had surmounted the eastern pine grove. Preparations had been underway for weeks and there was little for the ladies to do beyond making their best toilets.

"Nankeen pelisses are worn here for afternoons, aren't they Priscilla?" asked Polly Hayne and then bit her tongue at the implied reflection on Mecklenburg's taste.

Anne Rutledge was sure they were. Her own pelisse had an undervest of bright green satin and she was determined to wear it.

"Yes," laughed Priscilla, "when we have them. But don't expect to see the products of a Parisian mantua-maker. Most of our seamstresses are home trained. Actually our men are better dressed than our ladies since the tailors are usually white."

"Have you seen the accounts of Mme. Jerome Bonaparte's *costume de cour* in Washington?" asked Eliza Hampton. "I hear the longer she reigns the less she wears."

"I like Dolly Madison's clothes, myself," said Anne Rutledge, "especially those fetching turbans."

"Well, if Mrs. Adlai Osborne from Belmont were coming over," Priscilla added, "you'd see the *haut gout* of the west. But I'm afraid Iredell County is beyond our guest list."

She directed the house girls to lay out for the evening

the satins, silver lamés and embossed crapes of the modish trio and led the way down stairs.

The hill top soon filled with carriages, sulkies and saddle mounts, many of the ladies riding the last. There were as yet no chariots by Fielding of Philadelphia but on the whole Priscilla considered the equipages respectable.

With the exception of Colonel Brevard, General Graham and General Forney who had imported a personal tailor of their own from New York, all the gentlemen and a majority of the ladies wore the same finery in which they had appeared at Priscilla's wedding. But the materials were handsome if the styles less well-preserved, and the Charlestonians had not seen them before.

For the afternoon there was mint sling and blackberry acid. For the evening, peach brandy sweetened with honey, and cherry bounce made with black cherries, cloves and sugared rye. If the gentlemen preferred, they might have a straight dram with Alec in private. And the ladies who disapproved of any heightening of natural spirits were supplied with soft cider and lemonade, for which Alec consented to contribute some of his buried ice.

Had it not been for Captain Jamie McIntyre, a relic of the Revolution, Priscilla would have considered her day without a cloud. The old soldier had a natural aptitude for the inapt.

"Among our good farmers here," he told Priscilla's guests, "we have Hamptons, Rutledges and Haynes. Are they kin of yours?"

The girls weren't sure but said they hoped so.

Priscilla's father could have told her that the blood was probably the same. But somehow the question seemed a presumption on the part of the backwoods captain.

He wasn't finished yet. After hobbling over the house from basement to attic, he patted Alec familiarly on the back and observed:

"It's a long way you've come, my lad, since Jeremiah McIntosh."

Few people remembered that Jeremiah had had his passage paid from Scotland to Pennsylvania by a wealthy Quaker and had worked seven years in that colony to pay it back. It was no disgrace and many had come the same way.

"For myself," Priscilla had heard General Graham tell her father, "I admire a man more for making his own way." But Charleston preferred to forget. Maybe the Piedmont would too, in another generation.

"The one I'd forget," she had put in, "would be the father of the man who was subjected to such indignities."

"But don't overlook the fact," her own father had admonished her, "that many were poor for conscience sake. If the Huguenots hadn't been willing to suffer we'd still be under the tyranny of the Pope."

"Anytime," General Graham added, "that a man's convictions aren't stronger than his ambition, he's in a bad way. We had some pretty tempting offers from Cornwallis, you know."

"Would you rather be a rich McCafferty," brother Joe had asked, "or a poor Brevard?" Jeremiah McCafferty had turned Tory to save his property and after the war Charlotte had held him to account.

But all of this was ancient history and Priscilla didn't want to discuss it with Captain McIntyre. He was right.

It was a long way. She wondered if he meant to imply "too long a way." Probably not. An octogenarian could speak his mind without people taking offense. Just the same she wished he hadn't come.

Other visitors had shorter memories. The least present-able ones did, however, "cousin" her most profusely. Especially was this true of those who still lived in log houses. And a great many did.

"This place," one of them told her, "sure puts the brick houses of old Mr. Torrance, Dr. Joe Alexander and your grand-daddy in the shade." Since these were perhaps the best houses in Hopewell, the observation was obviously a compliment.

"You don't have to have brick," Priscilla answered mod-estly, "to have a nice home. I think Holly-wood, Latta Place and the Wilson homes are lovely." But as all of these were frame and not log, Priscilla's tact was not as effective as she had intended.

"They say General Bill Davie," continued her "cousin", "down about the Falls in South Carolina has got the finest house on the River."

"That's Tivoli," Priscilla agreed, "General Davie is a friend of father's and grandfather's but I've never seen his home."

"And do you know," her confidant whispered, "they say he uses china bowls for you-know-what instead of going out to the privy."

Priscilla did know as did most in the State since the political opponents of General Davie had widely pub-licized the innovation as an evidence of his aristocratic pretensions. She was thankful that none of her Charleston company was within earshot. Modern conveniences had not reached all of Mecklenburg but there was no use advertising the deficiency.

A third barbarian descended upon Priscilla. He was almost a professional fortune hunter. Being twice a widower and having run through the dowries of both wives, he was out for a third. If he couldn't get honey he'd take molasses, provided it was rich enough. Priscilla was in a pet to steer him away from the girls but he was obviously intent on gallantry.

Alec providentially was near by and sized up Priscilla's dilemma.

"Uncle Tom," he said leading by the arm the possessor of one of the Piedmont's most respected names, "you need a Curacoa cordial, I'm saving those for the gay Lotharios like yourself." "Uncle" Tom succumbed to the more immediate temptation, and Priscilla turned to find herself face to face with the Reverend Samuel Caldwell.

Despite his sermon on Sunday the minister gave the house his benediction on Monday.

"May the Lord increase your seed," he told his hostess, "like the sands of Jordan."

Priscilla's "Thank you" lacked warmth. From the distaff point of view the implications exceeded the honors.

"Seeds grow best," Dr. Joe Alexander put in a comforting aside, "when the field gets its seasons of fallow."

C H A P T E R 10

CLOUD OVER CATAWBA

At the end of the week Priscilla's friends took a tearful departure. One of the Alexander men was going to Charleston and agreed to accompany them on the stage. It was with regret and relief that Priscilla said goodbye. Few in the up-country graced gentillity like the Rutledges, Haynes and Hamptons, but being mistress of Priscilla's Price was a less gentle undertaking than she had anticipated.

Even a completely appointed mansion-house didn't run itself. Mrs. Brevard had a white housekeeper and Priscilla once suggested that her mother find another for her.

"When you are past fifty, have borne ten babies, and begin to fear sleepy staggers," her mother told her, "then you should employ a housekeeper. In the meantime with Jupiter as major-domo and Polly as chief cook I think Alec would be foolish to humor you."

Alec would have humored her for the asking, but since Priscilla's Price was set to her own scale she was ashamed to admit that she couldn't carry it alone.

The house servants consisted of nine women and three men. To personify the analogy of his Greek democracy, Alec jokingly called the women for the nine Muses, and the Negresses, nothing averse to the Olympian elevation, soon attached the names as due their positions. Polyhymnia was chief cook and Calliope her first assistant. Clio and Erato were seamstresses. Euterpe and Melpomene cleaned the first and second floors respectively. Terpsichore did the laundry. Thalia was Priscilla's personal maid and Urania was the "company girl" for guests.

Of the men, Jup, now cotton-pated and claiming to remember Governor Tryon, was responsible for the efficiency of the menage. Pluto had charge of the horses and drove the coach. "Gullah Jack," who came from Charleston and failed to fit into the mythological milieu, was yard boy with the care of the soap house, the smoke house and the privies.

Fortunately for Priscilla, her mother had laid the basis for adequacy in works along with her faith.

"A dash of Presbyterian directness," said Mrs. Brevard, "is an essential leaven for Huguenot confectionary." French people, she thought, spent too much time on decoration and too little on thoroughness. There was likely to be dust under the Aubusson carpet.

Priscilla found that definite instructions in the mornings gave her more leisure in the afternoons for embellishments. And it was the latter in which she delighted.

The gardens had yet to be laid out in parterres and the avenues planted. For her borders Priscilla had set her heart on English box. A burnt-house site of the Wilsons had the remains of an extensive maze and the Wilson cousins, prodigal and generous to their own undoing, gladly gave her all she chose to dig. English box was smaller leafed and fuller than the American variety.

On Alec's advice she designed her garden on the pattern of the Greek Key, which pleased his fancy and provided for her as many parterres as she wished. Priscilla decided upon four and amused herself by giving each a name and peculiar character.

"In the Bible Garden," she told Alec, "there will be only

flowers from the Scriptures: Roses of Sharon, Stars of Bethlehem, Jacob's ladders and a Judas tree.

"The Indian Garden is to have Cherokee plums, Indian pinks and a Catalpa tree, which, you know, was named for the Catawbas.

"There'll be a French Garden for the Brevards with mignonette, fleur-de-lis, golden immortelle and a crepe myrtle, which isn't really French but looks like it ought to be."

"And how about the McIntoshes?" Alec queried.

"Being Scotch, they're omitted to save you money," she laughed. "No, in honor of my lord I offer blue-bells, thrift and purple heather. I can't think of any tree but a Scotch pine."

Alec professed himself satisfied with the selection and obliged by the compliment.

For her avenues Priscilla sent Gullah Jack to the woods to dig honey locust shoots and wrote letters to friends in Brunswick County for magnolia seedlings. When she visited the quarters she intended to progress down an avenue of magnolias. The locusts were to be used for the path to the stables. From the house to the kitchen garden there would be rows of mimosa, a feathery tree from India which the Averys in Morganton had recently introduced.

"All very beautiful," Alec commented. "But do you realize, my sweet, that not one of your avenues provides any real shade?"

"Outside the house," Priscilla told him loftily, "a woman's function is to beautify. Practical defects are male problems."

The answer to this one Alec declared beyond his ken.

All of her whimsies amused him and he even consented to have trumpet vines and morning glories grow over the various outhouses.

Priscilla's planning was not without thought of the distant future. There were manor-houses in England and chateaux in France, she knew, which had stood for centuries and each generation had added a touch of its own personality. In time, no doubt, Priscilla's Price would rival the finest. It pleased her to think that as first chatelaine of the mansion she must eventually become a legend to her descendants. Not that she was impatient to join the ranks of ancestors, but the conviction gave an importance to her decisions.

Her most cherished dreams seemed sure of fulfilment. All she need do was enjoy the present. But it was sinful to feel too certain of prosperity. The rich man in Luke who grew vain of his possessions had lost his soul. Priscillia's conscience nagged her out of complacency. She was impatient for Alec's return and his diverting optimism.

Whether or not Priscilla was tempting Providence she was certainly overtaxing her strength. Mornings found her with a heavy weariness and a tendency to nausea. The signs were unmistakable. The forth-coming McIntoshes were apparently impatient to begin so idyllic an existence.

There was chicken-pox amongst the Brevard slaves, and Priscilla's mother and sisters were afraid to come and stay with her. She had missed the vexatious pox in childhood and it wasn't necessary for Aunt Polly in the kitchen to warn her that chicken-pox in the mother always deforms the unborn child.

Priscilla's maiden Aunt Sally at Rural Hill was available for emergencies. She had nursed many a youthful niece and nephew through poxes and fevers, had dressed the brides, admonished the grooms and regulated the fruits of their unions. Dr. Joe Alexander, who spoke with the authority of Princeton, said Aunt Sally had more sense in a sick room than a lot of doctors he knew. He admitted that sometimes she was a little pig-headed in obsolete prescriptions but most of them were harmless.

Like many of those whose name she shared, Aunt Sally was always right. And she could quote scripture to prove it. A little book called *Every Man His Own Doctor* printed in Salisbury back in 1798, had explained fully how the Lord had provided in every locality native simples to cure the disorders of that climate. The man who wrote it didn't know as much as Aunt Sally but he had the right idea. On every plantation there should be an herb garden, and since Priscilla had improvidently spent all of her time on flowers Aunt Sally brought the essential dried herbs with her and the roots of others to begin a prescription patch.

The darkies called Aunt Sally the "tea lady." For every internal ailment she could brew a sure-cure decoction. Peruvian bark was all right for malaria but not a whit more effective than boiled dog-wood berries. For winter colds, sage tea was best; for colic, catnip tea. Sweetgum tea would check diarrhea, and sassafras tea was a specific for bronchitis, pneumonia and measles. Any darkie who looked run down, and Aunt Sally's ministrations included all in the quarters, was sure to get a holly root tonic until he perked up again.

Alec had no objections to the old lady's company although he wearied occasionally of her endless Biblical repertoire. She knew the scriptures from Genesis to Revelation, the Holy Land from Dan to Beersheba, and the Lord's will from Alpha to Omega. Her total lack of humor provided her host with an entertaining foil and he scandalized her by observing that although she had created the Lord in her own image he thought it a very appropriate form for divinity. However, he saw to it that the McIntosh carriage was provided for her use at any time the doors of Hopewell opened.

Dr. Alexander called regularly once a month. That he could be reached in time for the delivery was improbable and was not considered essential unless Priscilla's labor was prolonged. He recommended a midwife of his acquaintance who could come for a week before the expected date and live in the house. To Aunt Sally the precautions were overdone.

"A few stiff teas," she insisted, "and cheerful conversation to prevent sinking of the spirits is all that any normally formed woman needs during childbirth."

But she was learning that with respect to Priscilla Alec overdid everything.

On each trip to Charlotte, Lincolnton or Salisbury, and he would not venture farther during his wife's confinement, Alec brought home silver spoons, cups, corals, pap-boots and any appropriate trinkets he could purchase in the general stores.

He exhausted the patience of the merchants in his demands for spermacetti candles as the burning of tallow and unsavory lard gave Priscilla the vapors.

Cornelia, one of the field hands who had recently produced a thriving pickaninny, was established in a yard cabin to replenish the milk supply.

When Priscilla's nine months were accomplished, the big house was in labor down to its rock foundations. Mrs.

O'Toole, the midwife, had been on hand for over a week and had received detailed instructions from Aunt Sally on how the women of her family always bore their babies.

"It's ignorant superstition," the spinster declared, "to place a knife under the bed to cut the pains. It's downright sacrilegious. My niece is fortified by her faith for any physical trials with which the Lord may see fit to test her."

Nevertheless, Mrs. O'Toole with less faith and more experience had carefully wrapped a cleaver and hidden it between the down and cotton mattresses.

Both guardians concurred in the belief that red pepper and ginger tea were essential to prevent a relaxing of the mother's efforts.

Priscilla was seized by a chilling fright. Not for the pain and not, she believed, for her life. She was frightened for the fate of her soul. To many young matrons of her acquaintance childbirth had brought fatal fevers. If her time had come, was she ready to meet her Maker? Alec had provided every luxury to ease her lot but he could not allay her fears. There had been no prayers together. He had thanked her, but not his God, for his good fortune and she had let it pass. Each labor contraction was a pitchfork of conscience. A strange time this to think of Peter McClelland but Priscilla tried to formulate in her mind the words of comfort he would assuredly have for a mother who died in labor.

She found it impossible to concentrate on the cheerful conversation of her two determined wardens. They were forced to content themselves with encouraging each other. As her pains increased she searched wildly about the room for a distraction. The ornately carved Elfe bedstead with

its side curtains of brocaded silk had once cheered her
heart. Damask window drapes and a Turkey carpet protected her from every fugitive draft. But these were cold
comfort now. The layette of the finest cambric, sheerest
batiste, and softest gauze was suited for a prince. But
what did it matter?

Priscilla must give birth with the same travail that black
Cornelia had suffered to bring forth the tiny slave now
set apart as body servant for the first heir of Priscilla's
Price. Child bearing was a great leveller. "God resisteth
the proud but giveth grace to the humble." Could she
count on His grace?

Her face and forehead were wet but through her mind
raced, not thoughts of her husband or of the life within
her but of her assets for salvation. Although she had missed meeting for the last few months, pregnancy was an
acceptable justification. She should have insisted that
Alec go. He was generous to the church. Next to the
Torrances his stipends for the preacher were the largest
at Hopewell. But had he sufficient faith? St. Paul had
written, "The unbelieving husband is sanctified by the
wife." God would not hold her accountable for Alec's
levity. She had been obedient to her husband. Was not
her present extremity proof of that? But was she humble?
Even Aunt Sally had not claimed that the Lord looked
with disfavor on those in high estate provided they came
by their riches through honest toil. Yet according to Mark
it was easier for a camel to go through the eye of a needle
than for a rich man to enter into the Kingdom of God.
A rich man or a woman . . . .

A violent tearing cut through her thoughts and she released her paroxysm in a scream. Her strength bolted

from her. About the room the old ladies moved like clouds in a hazy sky. Someone was rubbing her stomach, gently. She wondered, half dazed, if it were over. Then a lamb-like bleat broke the strange silence. Aunt Sally had laid on with a resolute palm. The first lungfull of Mecklenburg air was blown back into the room with a reverberating squall.

Mrs. O'Toole continued to massage Priscilla's abdomen. "Breathe hard in your hands," she commanded.

Priscilla struggled to comply and sensed a feeling of relief. She heard Aunt Sally say, "He looks like a McIntosh to me." Then she passed into welcome oblivion.

CHAPTER 11

CLOUD OVER CATAWBA

IF NOTHING in the Catawba Valley had been good enough for Priscilla before Alec married her, nothing in the twenty-one states exceeded her deserts after she bore him a son. He ordered a coach from Fielding in Philadelphia, and, as soon as Priscilla was able to travel, took her on a triumphal tour to the northward. Alexander, Jr., was left to the worshipful care of Cornelia under hawk-like supervision from Aunt Sally. The overseer was instructed to call at the big house twice daily and Dr. Joe Alexander agreed to stop in at least once a week whether summoned by Aunt Sally or not.

Philadelphia impressed Priscilla more than any city she saw. The Chestnut Street Theater surpassed even Broad Street's in Charleston, but the famous Christ Church was not to her thinking a near competitor in elegance to St. Michael's. In addition to the Theater, Mr. Peale's museum of marvels in Independence Hall proved a source of unending diversion to Alec and Priscilla. The Hall itself was hallowed by the historic Liberty Bell and mementoes of the presence there of George Washington. Priscilla knew that the Father of his Country had also visited Charlotte. She wondered what he had thought of the village after being in a metropolis of fifty thousand people. Fortunately, the first President's private journal was not made public for many years afterwards.

On their way home they stopped in the nation's capital, which Priscilla considered vastly inferior to Philadelphia. The Capitol building was still incomplete after its burning by the British in the late war. The huge vacant spaces left for future development gave the city an air of desolation. It was, as often observed by visitors, a city of magnificent distances. Only the President's palace, popularly called "The White House" was up to expectations. Priscilla thought that even it would be much improved with a portico.

The northern tour was but a beginning for Alec, and the following year they made a progress to the Virginia Springs. This time Cornelia and her black and white twins were taken along. Alec secured a cabin at the White Sulphur which was rapidly becoming the Bath of America. To Priscilla the social oligarchy of Singletons, Hamptons and Chestnuts was congenial company and Alec saw to it that there was nothing in homage rendered the greatest that was not also accorded his wife. Mr. Calwell, the proprietor, who wore his white hair in a cue tied with a black ribbon, was a despotic social arbiter. Unless the guests came well recommended and in their own carriage they were turned away to join the canaille at the Blue Sulphur. Despite its growing prestige, the White Sulphur's living accommodations were very primitive compared with Priscilla's Price. The McIntosh party considered its health restored after a two weeks cure.

During the year following this excursion, Priscilla was again "enceinte," as they said at the Springs. Aunt Sally had not yet concluded the visit which had begun with Alexander's arrival and rendered such valiant service that the new baby was named Sarah in her honor.

As her reward for this second contribution to Alec's posterity, Priscilla chose a trip to Charleston. Here she and her family spent a month at the Planters' Hotel. The unparalleled hospitality of the city by the sea to those it found acceptable made this the happiest of Priscilla's travels. Her seminary schoolmates were all married to their cousins, ensconced properly below Broad Street and resisting with futile contumacy the domination of their black domestics.

"This is a different world, isn't it?" Priscilla confided to Alec.

He agreed. "But I'd never feel at home here in less than a hundred years. You can't adopt Charleston. You have to inherit it. Or maybe it comes from eating rice."

"I didn't mean I wanted to move down," Priscilla smiled. "Instead of wishing we were a part of it we ought to encourage the prospects of Charlotte. After all, the Charlestonians began with a mud flat. We have a natural advantage."

"When steamships ply the Catawba," Alec remarked ruefully, "we may catch up with them. Wagons to market make slow progress." But nothing Priscilla could have said would have pleased him more. She had taken the thoughts from his mind. In appreciation, he had Charles Frazer do elegant miniatures of the two children.

The Mecklenburgers returned with heightened ambitions to their native hills. Low-country society was ruled by an educated aristocracy. Manigaults, Pinckneys and Middletons attended the College of Charleston, or at least its grammar school. In Lincolnton a movement was underway to establish a western college. A crude beginning, perhaps, but closer home than Chapel Hill. Alec signed up for a subscription when he learned that Dr. McRee, Colonel Thomas G. Polk and General Joseph Graham were among the trustees.

A new academy in Hopewell gave Priscilla an opportunity for munificent disposal of the histories of Dr. David Ramsay, preceptor of her Uncle Ephraim, which she had purchased in a moment of cultural enthusiasm in Charleston. Reverend John Williamson, the recently installed minister, and his wife were offering to take scholars.

Along with higher education, Alec believed, there should be an elevation of more of the farmers' sons to the status of planters. The Mecklenburg Agricultural Society gave silver cups and medals as prizes and Alec threw the weight of his influence with those members who were promoting the increasing cultivation of cotton.

"If the nationalists don't tie us with tariffs," he prophesied, "there's no reason why the South can't supply the world with cotton. There are fortunes there as well as in rice and indigo."

Although he found as little sport in lotteries as he did in cockmains, most of the former were sponsored by respectable charities and Alec religiously bought tickets. When he approved the benefits he did not attend the drawings but turned over his tickets to the sponsors. In a section where few had surplus capital, small contributions from the many willing to take a chance were not repugnant even to church proprieties.

Colonel Thomas G. Polk, Dr. Thomas Henderson, Robert Wilson and others were importing pedigreed stallions to improve their saddle and racing stock.

"Within a few years," Alec told one of the Charleston Haynes who had married a Mount Tirzah cousin of Priscilla's, "your Washington Course will have to look to its laurels."

"We anticipate the competition," the Low-countryman assented. "I have seen by your papers that Florizel,

Napoleon and Fancier have stood in Mecklenburg."

"Also Palifox and Mississippi," Alec added. "Wild Medley will stand at Major Morrow's shortly. He was bred by Captain Samuel Washington of Virginia and has been let to mares here often in the past. Stud fees this year are ten dollars the season or six the single leap."

"That doesn't seem high for a racer," Hayne observed.

"For myself," said Alec, "I'm not breeding for the turf. But a strain of the Arabian Godolphin improves any man's stable."

The day following he had the overseer take over the best selection of his mares. He also sent the coach. Aaron Wheeler had set himself up as "Coach, Sign and Ornamental Painter" in the village. And Priscilla was ambitious to have the family look its best at the coming anniversary of the twentieth of May.

May 20th, 1825, was Mecklenburg's biggest celebration to date. Fifty years had elapsed since the County's patriots had published their radical resolutions. The Mecklenburg Declaration of Independence was accepted by the nation as an important historical event. Until a dispute six years past between the Congressmen of Virginia and Massachusetts had brought Mecklenburg's prior claim to the country's attention, Charlotte had done little to advertise her distinction. But now that the lowly Tar-heels had discomforted both proud pretenders, it was time for self-congratulation in Mecklenburg.

To mark the coming of age in the saddle of Alexander, Junior, his father permitted him to ride in to Charlotte beside the freshly painted coach. Alexander had been presented with Alec's faithful Meg on his seventh birthday. From her high eminence as the dappled filly of the paddock, Meg had descended to old grey mare. But her disposition had likewise toned down to a soberer hue.

Scipio, Alexander's shadow, by a fruitful providence out of Cornelia, was given a mule. Owing to similarly doubtful origins, the mule was known as Mixtry. No other darkey on the place had a mount of his own and Scipio's future as body servant to the Master was clearly proclaimed by the distinction. Except for Spring ploughing, when Mixtry was temporarily pressed into service, Scipio was as much the mounted monarch of the quarters as was Alexander amongst his contemporaries of the River plantations.

The youthful horsemen pranced their steeds on either side of the double span of bays. It was a great day. Pluto was perched high on the driver's seat with Cornelia at his side. Inside the coach rode Alec, Priscilla, Sarah (aged three) and Aunt Sally. The last was now a permanent convert to the superiority of Priscilla's Price over the mellowed elegance of Rural Hill.

"It's a pity the doubting Thomases can't be here today," Aunt Sally opined. "There'll be dozens of citizens present who were eyewitnesses fifty years ago. If the Congressmen used their ears they'd have less trouble with their understandings."

"After the evidence printed by the State," observed Alec, "I thought all unbiased critics had conceded Mecklenburg's claims."

"All with their wits have," Aunt Sally rejoined. "Personally, Pa's word is good enough for me. I do wish he had taken me along with him. I was fifteen at the time and I never forget anything important."

"Then, why," Alec teased, "did you make that list of things you wanted to do in Charlotte?"

"Fiddlesticks, young man," Aunt Sally retorted, "I do that to impress my memory. Then I forget the list. Here, you take it." She began to itemize her missions for the day:

"I am going first to Smith and Carson's to get a copy of *The Southern Preacher*. Many of the sermons are by ministers I have heard in the flesh." Not since she bought MacWhorter's *Sermons* had Aunt Sally owned a book by a personally acquainted author. The *Catawba Journal* and the Salisbury papers printed pamphlets by local aspirants but Aunt Sally liked the dignity of a calfskin binding.

"Then I am going to hunt up the Reverend Samuel Caldwell," she continued. "He may know something about this new Sunday School Society. If it's a movement that will last I'll see that Mr. Williamson gets it started at Hopewell."

"What next?" Alec glanced at the paper.

"A Cashmere shawl at Samuel McComb's. They're said to be lighter than Paisley's. Made from goats in India. It's McComb's business to have them.

"And last to William Culverhouse's to look at Windsor chairs and a settee for Priscilla. She has other things to do."

"Well, that's a full day," Alec agreed. "And I'll concede you *mens sana in corpore sano* as Preacher Caldwell used to say." He turned to his wife. "What's keeping you so busy, Priscilla?"

"Not much, really," she laughed. "The *Journal* office is advertising Dutch and Opaque quills and we need some.

I'd like to find out if Aaron Wheeler can paint anything besides signs and coaches. I noticed the Charlestonians hang oil paintings of historical events."

"The signing of our declaration," Aunt Sally interrupted, "would be an excellent subject."

"So it would," Priscilla agreed, "if he can do it. But most of all, Alec, I want to find out when the Thalian Association is giving a play."

"Our theater on Trade Street won't be much," Alec mused, "after those on Broad and Chestnut. I'm for it though. We've got to encourage home talent. Even at the cost of a dull evening."

"And what's on your roster, Mr. McIntosh," Aunt Sally queried.

"Do you really want to know?"

"I asked you, young man."

"John McQuay's grog shop is first. Now don't ruffle your feathers. I only want some rum to mix with molasses so the quarters can celebrate 'Independency' when we get home. Of course, if I get in and out of the shop without a gouging, I'll be surprised."

"Alec," remembered Priscilla, "you must go by William Smith's and have a fitting for another broadcloth coat."

"I will, sweetheart, and I'll have to include a call at the Newbern bank on Tryon and cash this draft from our Charleston factor if I expect to pay today's bills."

Consideration of finances mildly irritated Priscilla. "We really need a new coach," she announced. "I wouldn't be surprised if the Alexanders, Springs' and Torrances haven't imported new ones from Philadelphia."

"We can look in on J. G. Morse," Alec replied unperturbed. "I think he is still at his stand across from the Theater. He's made the best coaches in the county for a good many years."

"Oh, let's not get a homemade one, Alec," Priscilla looked alarmed. "I believe in trading in Charlotte, of course, but we have to keep up appearances. For the children, I mean. This one is only six years old. Maybe if we had the McIntosh arms on the panel, like the Osbornes, it would do all right."

Alec was averse to that species of ostentation.

"We'll see what the Polks have," he side-stepped tactfully. The family intended to spend the night at the home of Colonel Thomas G. Polk a few miles east of the village. There was no name more honored in the county than Polk but not many of that ilk indulged themselves without returns on the investment.

"I wonder how the cotton stands east of Charlotte," Alec continued. "Ours has had too much rain this year. But we can't let up. I'm confident Colonel Tom will second my efforts to encourage expansion. The Polks have a keen eye for the future."

"Yes," chuckled Aunt Sally, "when both your Colonel Tom's father and grandfather courted Sister Rebecca at the same time, Pa said it was a sure sign we had arrived in the world."

The straggling little village loomed up in the distance. Alec knew by name all thirty of the white families residing there and by sight a majority of its seven hundred inhabitants, slaves included. The wealth of the county was not in the town, and the office holders generally lived on their plantations nearby. Townspeople were commonly merchants and mechanics and not too prosperous.

CHAPTER 12

CLOUD OVER CATAWBA

DESPITE ITS MODEST commerce, the Charlotte of 1825 showed a material improvement over that of the historical event it celebrated. Fifty years before, the county Whigs in log and rock houses had repudiated the King of England and his homely spouse for whom their seat was named. The village now boasted three substantial buildings of brick, the church on East Trade, the jail on North Tryon and the courthouse on the Square.

The day was fair but the roads were still rutted from the rains and the wheels of the McIntosh coach had difficulty keeping in the grooves. An occasional hog defied its progress. At the increasing evidence of civilization, the horses pricked their ears and strained to canter up Trade Street. They passed vehicles of infinite variety bringing in the equally various citizenry of the County.

"You'll have to admit," Alec pointed out a conspicuous brick edifice with a low belfry, "that that isn't a bad church for a town this size."

"For elegance," Priscilla commented, "it needs a spire. I don't see why Presbyterians and spires are so incompatible."

"Because Roman cathedrals have spires," Aunt Sally stated.

"Because steeples cost money," Alec corrected her. "The time will come, if the Lord continues to prosper the Presbyterians, when we'll not only have steeples but stained glass, artificial music and even a vested choir."

"Perish the day," Aunt Sally ejaculated, "and you with it for your impiety."

A little further on the coach passed old Cooks Tavern, a two-story wooden building with a long piazza and balcony. It was partly shaded by a row of large China trees. Here George Washington had lodged on his Southern Tour after the Revolution. There had been no church then and only a plank courthouse on high brick pillars. No wonder the President confided to his journal that Charlotte was "a trifling place."

"Now to me," Priscilla observed, as they reached the Square, "the courthouse is much more impressive than the church. The cupola gives it some distinction." Beneath the cupola was a square brick building with a hipped roof. Since 1810, it had served all community purposes for the village.

"Doesn't it offend your conscience, Aunt Sally," Alec commented, "that before the church was built all the preaching in town was done on the ground floor of the courthouse and all the public balls held on the second?"

"Those primitive days," Aunt Sally enlightened him, "have passed. Besides, the best people in town belonged to Mr. Caldwell's congregation at Sugaw Creek. They were closer to a church than you are now."

"It's a pretty gay town even yet," said Alec, refusing to rise at her aspersion.

Despite a lack of paint and polish, Charlotte had acquired a reputation for elaborate dinners and evening parties. Travellers passing through made note of the fact in their diaries.

"I wish Pa had been as modern as the Wilsons," Priscilla mused, "and let us come in to Charlotte for the balls. The

Wilsons always have had more of the *joie de vivre* than anybody in Mecklenburg."

Aunt Sally, though half a Wilson, gave a snort. "If our cousins," she remarked, "were as much concerned with their church as they are with their horses and hounds, Hopewell would have a new house of worship today."

No one mentioned the black sheep of the family. But it was commonly believed that if Ben Wilson had not been in some way involved in Nixon Curry's slave stealing ring the latter would not have shot him. The murder was still fresh in Mecklenburg's mind, but Curry had escaped to the West. Digging in the mire might raise more snakes than could be laid.

As the coach jolted down South Tryon Street, Alec pointed out the sites for the proposed male and female academies to which he had contributed.

"It might be well," he suggested, "to send Alexander and Sarah in for a few terms."

"I doubt they'll be finished in time," Priscilla observed hurriedly. "And anyway I think we owe them a better start than will likely be available here. Aunt Sally has offered to teach Sarah until she is ready to go to Charleston or Philadelphia."

"I don't pretend to be a scholar," Aunt Sally began modestly, "but I wrote a better hand than most of the boys in the Old Field school."

"Sarah will be the envy of her sex," Alec remarked truthfully, "if she grows up with the accomplishments of her namesake." He didn't mention what the men might think.

"How about Western College for Alexander?" he suggested hopefully.

"It's all right to educate the boys at home," Priscilla conceded. "But he'll need a tutor first. And Lincolnton is a long way from getting the college started."

"It's a pity," Alec mused, "that Charlotte lacked the enterprise to re-establish old Queens. We'd have the oldest college south of Virginia. An institution that trained men like General Jackson, Governor Davie and General Graham must have had its points." All that was left of it was the wreck of a frame building which Dr. Thomas Henderson had moved across to his lot and now used as a barn.

"I'm glad the College Green is left," Priscilla commented. "We should have come in for the May Day ceremony there. I saw in the *Catawba Journal* that Elizabeth Henderson was crowned queen with amateur musicians, a piano and dances on the Green by the queen and her train."

"Just think," Alec taunted, "if you'd grown up in Charlotte you would certainly have been Queen on the Green."

Aunt Sally sniffed. "And have her name in the public prints? I should hope not!"

Priscilla ignored them both. "The Princeton boys call their Green the 'Campus.' That's rather elegant, I think."

Pluto reined in the horses before a large white house at the end of South Tryon Street. For the day, Dr. Thomas Henderson had invited the McIntoshes to make his home their headquarters.

All were in high activity at the Doctor's. He was host for the big dinner to be served in the Green grove. It was now ten o'clock and the procession was to form at eleven. After a quick splash at the commode basin and a generously declined offer to aid the Hendersons, Alec, Priscilla and Aunt Sally were off to their several errands. The children remained with Cornelia to watch the setting up of the long tables. In a matter of minutes they were lost in a covey of carefree pickaninnies. Pluto worked himself into a lather grooming the carriage quad for the parade.

At eleven sharp, the procession formed at the court-house. Colonel Thomas G. Polk was the central figure, as had been his paternal grandfather half a century before. Leading the procession were the cavalry and the Lafay-ette Artillery. Next followed citizens and strangers. Last marched the chief exhibits of the day, the Revolutionary veterans, some sixty or seventy strong, each wearing a badge stamped " '75."

The parade progressed down West Trade Street to the Presbyterian church. Though considered spacious, the building was soon packed to the doorjams. But as guests of the Hendersons and Polks, the McIntosh cortege was assured of a pew.

"The right people to know," Priscilla mused wisely, "are determined by place as well as position."

The Reverend Humphrey Hunter of Steele Creek opened the meeting with prayer.

"He must be all of seventy," Priscilla calculated. Her first recollections of Unity retained the awesome image of Dr. Hunter in the pulpit. She shivered a little.

The aged divine was gentler now but still no compro-miser. Next to the Holy Writ the words of the 20th of May bore for him the most positive evidence of literal inspira-tion. His prayer was followed by appropriate music from the band. He then read his county's Declaration of In-dependence.

"Fifty years ago," he announced solemnly, "I heard this same document proclaimed from the courthouse steps."

Colonel Thomas Polk, the orator of that occasion, now rested in the churchyard behind them.

The highlight of the day followed. Young Washington Morrison, recently home from Chapel Hill, delivered the congratulatory address. So appropriate and pathetic were his sentiments that tears trickled down the furrowed cheeks of the veterans. He extolled their patriotism, their privations without complaint and the freedom they had conferred on their fellow citizens. In a few short years, as well they knew, they would all be gone, but their legacy would live forever with a liberty-loving people.

Music and discharges from the cannon followed his peroration. To Alec, the less emotional address Dr. Winslow Alexander had given the year before at Hopewell was more to his taste. But Washington Morrison had caught the temper of the day. If the young man lived the plaudits of the Piedmont were his.

At four o'clock a large concourse sat down in the grove of the College Green. For many of the veterans, Dr. Henderson's appetizing spread rivalled Mr. Morrison's eulogy in satisfaction. General George Graham, brother of General Joseph, officiated as President, and Isaac Alexander, Esq., was Vice President.

After the cloth was removed, the toasts were drunk. Thirteen prearranged healths were offered and the table was thrown open for volunteers. As Alec had feared, politics then reared its ugly head. Where all had been harmony before, division was now rife.

Ex-Congressman William Davidson insisted on drinking to Henry Clay, but Colonel Polk quickly countered with a parody from "The Lady of the Lake:"

"To the political prospects of Henry Clay:
  Like the dew on the mountains
    Like the foam on the river
  Like the bubble on the fountain
    They are gone forever."

Henry W. Connor tried to get back to history with a toast to General William Lee Davidson, now safely dead these forty odd years. But J. H. Blake dug up Clay again.

With considerable tact, Captain T. I. Polk proposed anonymously: "The next President of the United States. May he be the choice of the people and not of Congress."

L. H. Alexander voiced the obvious when he followed with "Andrew Jackson." Many Mecklenburgers felt that the friend of all and the classmate of some on the very College Green on which they sat had got a raw deal from Congress. The Representatives may have preferred the icy John Q. Adams, but the people's choice was "Old Hickory." And elect him they would in '28. Henry Clay had queered his chances when he threw his influence to Adams and was appointed Secretary of State. To the Jacksonites, the people had been defrauded by a political "corrupt bargain."

The late May sun was beginning to wane as the McIntosh coach headed out East Trade toward the plantation of Colonel Thomas G. Polk. The day had been a glorious success.

"There are enough niggers in town," Dr. Henderson had observed to Alec, "to pay all the debts of Henry Clay himself."

The only somber note in the paean of rejoicing had been a warning from Dr. Joe Alexander. "Awful lot of people together," he remarked portentously, "considering the amount of smallpox in the South last year."

He had previously suggested to Alec that he have the children inoculated with cowpox as a preventive. Priscilla might have consented but for the tragedy in Nash and Edgecomb Counties four years before. Almost all of the people inoculated had developed actual smallpox. In vain the physicians explained that a tragic error had occurred. Smallpox crusts had been mailed by mistake for vaccine fluid. Whatever the cause the horror shocked the country and the postal laws permitting free passage of vaccine fluid had been repealed.

Colonel Polk arrived at home before his guests. Willswood was not a show place. It had been inherited from the incumbent's father and evinced the simplicity of an earlier era. The high frame building was without ornamentation and hardly up to the position occupied by the family it housed. Considering their affluence, Priscilla thought they might have done as well as Archibald Frew who had built an arresting home on the Salisbury Road. But the Polks were men for the main chance, and spending money on houses in Mecklenburg wasn't the way to get ahead in '25. Already most of the family had moved to Salisbury and Raleigh where prospects were more promising.

Willswood hospitality, however, was beyond cavil, and Mrs. Polk invited her guests into the domicile's great parlour whose wainscoting, mantel and cornice amply redeemed the plainness of its exterior. In the small withdrawing room, Alec and Colonel Tom were soon engrossed in the merits of sandy soil over blackjack for cotton and kept the house boy busy with a pitcher of toddy. Left alone, the McIntosh and Polk ladies dissected with delectable horror those of their dearest friends whose addiction to the snuff brush could not be confined to the privacy of unmixed gatherings. The Quaker meeting was only adjourned when candles were lighted and the servants brought supper from the yard.

CLOUD OVER CATAWBA

ON HER RETURN to the country, Priscilla was haunted by Dr. Alexander's grim warning. Of all plagues, and there were many, smallpox was the most pitiless. When it left life it left its victims branded, an object of revulsion or compassion for the rest of their lives. Priscilla remembered Alec's wistful mother.

She watched her son and daughter from the parlour window. With them were Scipio and a pickaninny whose head was matted with tight little pigtails indicating the female sex. The four were intent on a game of hopscotch with green maypops. Alexander had escaped the awkwardness common to boys his age and Sarah's blond curls darted about like yellow butterflies. Both were storybook children. Their complexions were as luminous and their colorings as vivid as those in their Frazer miniatures.

Priscilla's portrait, with the miniatures on either side, hung over the Duncan Phyfe sideboard in the dining room. There was another of an ancestress of Alec's by one of the Peales. Family portraits, according to Alec, should always hang in the dining room. Strangers were received in the parlour, but whom the family wished to take to its heart it brought to its board.

On an impulse Priscilla put down her petit point frame and needles, left the parlour window, and went back to look at the pictures. An oval mirror in a companion gilt frame balanced Priscilla's portrait on the opposite wall. From the mirror a reflection as flawless as the canvas colors returned her gaze. Priscilla felt a glow of gratification. After eight years there was no fading in the bloom

she had worn on the day Dr. McRee had joined her life to
Alec's. And her husband was as vain of her looks as he
was of the children's. Would he cease to love her if she
looked like his mother?

"Dear God," she breathed, "don't let that happen to us."

The great Family Bible caught her eye as she returned
to the parlour. Many Christians believed that in times of
crisis you could open the Book at random for a sign. But
even Dr. McRee told her that he thought this a superstition. There was nothing in the Scriptures to support it.
Nevertheless, the daily reading of the Holy Writ was prescribed by all the ministers.

As she lifted the heavy volume it fell open to the center.
Priscilla began to read in Isaiah 3. At the sixteenth verse
her heart beat faster.

Moreover, the Lord saith, Because the daughters of
Zion are haughty, and walk with stretched forth necks
and wanton eyes, walking and mincing as they go,
and making a tinkling with their feet:
Therefore the Lord will smite with a scab the crown
of the head of the daughters of Zion . . . .

She shut the book hastily. "It was an accident," she
assured herself. Alec would laugh it away. She wasn't
wanton. No one had ever accused her of being haughty,
not to her face. And when had she ever walked with
"tinkling feet"?

On Alec's return she did not mention the omen. It was
best forgotten. But he brought up the smallpox himself.

"Spring is the season when it usually begins," he remarked. "To be on the safe side, suppose Alexander and
I take the cowpox inoculation?"

Priscilla hesitated.

"You girls can try it when we get through. After all," he laughed "you've got more to your fortune than your face. We'll move down with Riley during the incubation."

Enough clothes to last for two weeks were carried to the overseer's log house. It was obvious from Riley's unappealing physiognomy that he had already had the disease.

Dr. Joe Alexander rode over in his sulky the following day and scratched in the poison. Aside from a light diet, plenty of liquids, and precautions against becoming overheated, no interruptions of their usual routines were prescribed.

Priscilla and Sarah waved to them each day as they rode below the house by the River. Sarah appeared completely lost without Alexander. When she wasn't listless she was fretful.

"It isn't like her," Priscilla thought, "but it's the first time they've been separated."

The baby took longer afternoon naps and had to be waked for supper. She showed no interest in her food in spite of her namesake's coaxing.

"Never saw a child more doted on her brother," Aunt Sally observed a little too obviously. "Of course, I was just as fond of Brother Robin. By the by, Priscilla, don't you think it's time Sarah began saying 'Brother Alexander'? Or do you think their ages are close enough to omit the formality? Ma was always very particular with us about it."

But Priscilla wasn't listening. The passage from Isaiah would give her no peace. How else could "Smite with a scab" be interpreted? Should she talk with Mr. Williamson? Perhaps Peter McClelland would have an explanation. But he had gone to Tennessee. Where could she turn?

On the fourth day after their return from the Charlotte celebration, Sarah began to complain of a pain in her back. Her eyes and cheeks were unnaturally bright. She wanted to go to bed.

Priscilla dismissed her nurse and took the child to her room. With weak fingers she unbuttoned her dress. On her face and neck the tiny flea bites were beginning to appear. Priscilla closed her eyes and prayed.

"Please, God, it can't be."

Sarah was fretful at her mother's delay and grew warm with impatience. Priscilla looked again with wide eyes and a tight throat. There was no room for doubt.

The baby cried out loud and brought Aunt Sally from her room. Priscilla lay unconscious on the floor.

There wasn't much Aunt Sally could do but she wasn't afraid. Dr. Thomson's *Family Physician* was almost as familiar to her as her Bible, but with respect to her namesake the latter was the safest guide. While she worked she made supplications for strength. How she did it she never knew but before Dr. Alexander arrived she had Priscilla and Sarah in bed in separate rooms. Sarah she put in her own big four poster as the trundle bed was too narrow for the tossing infant. With respect to personal danger, she breathed a hasty "Thy will be done" and forgot it. As much barley water and balm tea as the two patients would drink was poured down them. Priscilla might not need it but it wouldn't hurt.

Alec was sent for. He was in the bottoms and could not immediately be found. When he arrived his face was colorless and there was on him the strong odor of horse sweat. He had little to say.

Dr. Joe made no attempt to minimize the facts.

"It won't be necessary to give her ipecac. The eruption is coming out faster than it should for four days. Keep the room cool, continue the liquids, and give her acid fruits, such as cooked apples and preserved cherries. In case she continues restless, a teaspoon of syrup of poppies every five hours.

"Might as well do the same for Priscilla, although I see no signs of disorder except a failing of her constitution owing to anxiety."

Aunt Sally's faith augmented her aging vitality. She only left Sarah's side to see that the decoctions were properly prepared. The servants were useless in their herdlike fear. Jupiter called a prayer-meeting in the quarters when the hands got in from the fields. Their wailing chants could be heard at the house. Alec started to send Scipio to stop it, but thought better.

For two days Priscilla could not pull herself together. Aunt Sally kept her from Sarah lest her hysterical crying, which her efforts to control only heightened, frighten the child. Twice when Priscilla had started from her bed, she had fainted before reaching Aunt Sally's door. On recovering consciousness she retched in agony. Alec encouraged her to stay quiet in bed as long as possible. He hoped to keep her from seeing the child, though it was a senseless protection.

Aunt Sally's room gave off the peculiar nauseous oder

of the pox. On the third day Priscilla got herself under control, and dry-eyed, took charge.

Sarah's primary fever scarcely abated for the secondary. Purple and black spots began to appear amongst the pustules which were watery and running together. To prevent the baby from scratching, which deepened the scars, Alec, Priscilla and Aunt Sally took turns holding her hands. None of them could bear to have her arms bound down.

The purple and black spots, Dr. Alexander said, indicated a putrefaction of the blood. For this only Peruvian bark was effective and as much was given as Sarah could retain. In most cases it was advisable to open the pustules and let out the noxious matter. It helped to prevent pitting, but Sarah's sores were not of the hopeful firm variety.

As the primary fever passed into the secondary, the child's pulse became quick, her breathing laborious and her body heat intense. She weakened rapidly on the ninth day. Conscious that Aunt Sally was saying her prayers, Sarah made an effort to force "Now I lay me" through her swollen lips. It was beyond her strength. Alec and Priscilla knelt by her bed as she left them.

"The Lord gave and the Lord hath taken away, blessed be the name of the Lord."

Priscilla had moved in a coma. Only by deadening her senses could she force her body to perform its functions. Incoherent, formless prayers had floated unceasingly through her mind. She had never seen smallpox before. When she looked at the pestilent, noisome form which once had been a bright-faced child she did not associate it with her daughter. To Priscilla, Sarah had gone days before she ceased to breathe. It was unthinkable that the baby should grow up any way but lovely and whole. Priscilla did not feel it a blessing that Sarah died. She did not feel at all. A wall against reality forced itself up in her mind.

Her numbness lasted through the brief ceremony at the plantation burying-ground. She did not shed a tear. For twenty-five years she had been protected from the starkness and horror of physical suffering. She had no defenses. Father and husband had meant it as a kindness. Perhaps it had been for the best. Nothing in the past could alter the fact of the present. She did not seek strength, only oblivion.

Days passed but she failed to rally from her torpor. Within a week her color returned, but it was not the hue of health. The red eyes came not from tears, nor the drowsiness from resignation. She had neither. Before Dr. Alexander told them, both Alec and Aunt Sally knew. If Priscilla revived sufficiently to know she had the pox she would not try to live. The coma, said Aunt Sally, was a Godsend.

Priscilla's was not a virulent case. The pustules on her face were small and firm. Dr. Alexander opened them with his lancet and believed the scars would be slight. Something in her delirium fought against the disease. For two weeks she breathed without moving and swallowed the gruels, lemon juices and spirits of nitre without resistance. Instead of opiates, Dr. Joe recommended cordials. Poultices of mustard seed, oatmeal and vinegar were applied to her feet and hands to draw the humourous toward the extremities. She made no effort to claw the scabs.

When she regained consciousness, she was too weak to know what had passed. Her strength returned slowly as did her awareness of the world about her.

Aunt Sally thanked God when she saw tears roll from her niece's closed eyelids and heard her murmur "Sarah." Priscilla McIntosh was resigned to living.

CHAPTER 14

CLOUD OVER CATAWBA

TIME PROVED no healer to Priscilla.

When Alexander McIntosh, Junior, passed from uncertainty to manhood in his middle teens, he was so handsome that his mother was afraid to look at him. If she humored her eyes for more than a few seconds pride would well up within her.

Priscilla was persuaded that pride had stricken her down in the death of her daughter. Often she questioned the Reverend John Williamson at Hopewell. On the point of material possessions, which no longer interested Priscilla, the pastor could give her comfort. It was not the accumulation but the satisfaction of worldly goods that constituted sinful pride. Mr. Williamson had erected a brick mansion-house second to few in his congregation and operated profitably a large plantation. Temporal prosperity was becoming the reward of the just in the Catawba Valley.

With respect to Priscilla's soul-searching, Mr. Williamson left her in doubt. "God's ways are inscrutable to man. It is not for us to question or comprehend them." While he would not openly avow that Priscilla's ordeal was sent for her sins, he had no doubt that God had sent it.

Priscilla couldn't take a chance. If pride in any guise was the cause of her sufferings she must rend it from her. The only path she knew to a contrite spirit was the road to the church. Old Aunt Sally, now gathered to her fathers in Rural Hill burying-ground, had been the first at Hopewell when its doors opened. Priscilla was there to open the doors. Aunt Sally was a pale shadow of the faith compared with her niece's complete unification with it.

When funds were being solicited for the new brick meetinghouse in the early '30's, Priscilla had Pluto hitch up the coach and drive her to the home of every wealthy widow and spinster in the congregation. To approach the gentlemen would have been unseemly in her sex, but she used her influence to enlist aid from Alec. As a result of such efforts, and the good price on cotton, Hopewell built the finest house of worship in Mecklenburg. The elegance of its circular pulpit on an eight foot marbleized column was not looked upon as a worldly vanity since it was erected to the glory of God.

In Charlotte the Reverend Mr. Leavenworth was holding "prayer meetings" on Friday nights and conducting a "monthly concert of prayer for missions." Priscilla had avoided the town with its influx of recent settlers and their mundane amusements, but Mr. Leavenworth's ministrations brought her in whenever the roads were passable. She was unable to induce Alec to join the Bible Society for spreading the Word but he gave her money to contribute and put his name on the roll of the local Benevolent Society for home charities. With respect to the Sons of Temperance, who in violation of their titular profession usually demanded total abstinence, Alec agreed with General Joseph Graham: They were safe for the sons but fatal for the fathers. Only in the case of Foreign Missions did Alec fail to give Priscilla nominal support, although he observed in private that they were commendable in getting out of the country a lot of unpalatable relatives.

For over a year Alec had assumed that Priscilla's absorption in religion was temporary. He attributed it partly to a recoiling from the world owing to the blight of small-pox. Yet Priscilla was very lightly marked. Six feet away the scars were not visible. Her inversion went deeper than that. The shock of grief had produced an emotional menopause. She was no longer a whimsical girl, but a woman whose hopes were centered in the hereafter.

"It's lucky we aren't Romanists," he attempted to divert her, "or you'd desert me for the veil." But Priscilla failed to respond to his humor.

So complete an abnegation of the good things of this life seemed close to morbidity to Alec. He tried to interest Priscilla in the growing gaiety of the village.

"Less than ten years ago," he told her, "if my memory is as good as Aunt Sally's, you were complaining that Charlotte lacked the *joie de vivre*. Let me read you what your cousin James Graham writes about it today.

Recent settlers are becoming so numerous as to give a tone and new direction to the manners and customs, and instead of the notions and habits of the Scotch-Irish, which were about as stiff and unyielding as the blackjacks of their own soil, you now begin to look upon the polish and refinement of French Society.

"It seems very odd to me," Priscilla commented, "that Cousin James should be throwing off in print on the Scotch-Irish. He's certainly one of them."

"Oh, that wasn't for print," laughed Alec, "he's too good a politician for that. It's in a letter he wrote his famous brother William A. A public man shouldn't leave his mail on the tavern mantel if he doesn't want it read. I won't tell you who copied it out, but it wasn't I."

Priscilla smiled. "I didn't suspect you. You must feel guilty for reading it. As a matter of fact, I hear a good deal about Charlotte's 'French Society' without having to read other people's letters. At the Wilsons Monday the topic at dinner was the last ball. Cynthia presented me with the bill of fare." She took a paper from her reticule on the sewing table. "Wing of turkey, jelly, macaronies and mottoes, pickled oysters, *a la mode* beef, olives, lemonade, champagne, *blancmange,* ice cream, floating island, truffles and bons. And during the evening our cousins danced cotillions, contradances, mazourkas and gallopades!"

Alec grinned. "Well, I wasn't advocating that we go in for anything as strenuous as that. But I wish you'd think about taking in the twentieth of May. We'll skip the ball if you say, but I believe you'd enjoy the orations."

Priscilla didn't commit herself. Her interest in Mecklenburg's claim to distinction had considerably abated. It seemed to her that the few remaining Revolutionary veterans talked too much about their exploits in the past and not enough about their prospects for a future life.

In the mail which Alec had brought were the weekly issues of *The Charleston Observer,* a Presbyterian paper, and *The Christian Advocate,* published in Philadelphia. Priscilla read little else.

"I believe I'll look over the church papers," she told Alec. Customarily Priscilla clipped out the pieces of particular appeal after her second or third reading.

"Of making many scrapbooks," she mused, "there seems to be no end. Yet I cannot consider it a vanity to preserve these beautiful thoughts for the future. Someday, I pray God, Alexander and his children may gain comfort from them."

"I hope so," Alec replied and stifled a retort on Alexander's future behind his copy of *Niles Register*.

For the new novels of Sir Walter Scott, now all the vogue with the Southern feudalists, Priscilla had little time. The shocking Lord Byron whom she had slyly read in her teens was no longer a temptation. Alec sometimes read aloud passages from Robert Burns which pleased her (he usually selected those which erred on virtue's side) but her own poetry reading was confined to the solacing rhythms of Isaac Watts and Charles Wesley. To Priscilla "When I Survey the Wondrous Cross" was better poetry than "Childe Harold's Pilgrimage," and "Jesus, Lover of My Soul" of greater inspiration than "Don Juan."

Alexander, too, must be strengthened in the nurture and admonition of the Faith. After the boy had recited the Shorter Catechism, Priscilla encouraged him to learn the Larger one and many a Sunday afternoon they struggled together over the vagaries of the Westminster divines.

Had the plantation, bank stock, iron foundry and real estate been hers, Priscilla could gladly have sold it all and given to the poor. But for Presbyterian wives the husband was the head of the house and St. Paul had not authorized a questioning of what Alec did with his own.

When Alec became convinced that Priscilla's metamorphosis was permanent, he resolved to reconcile himself to the change. The McIntosh men were Stoics. What had happened had happened, and emotional rebellions were bad for both dignity and digestion. He did not love Priscilla less deeply, only less intensely. A part of her that had been his had died. She was readier to give, readier to acquiesce than ever. But her husband believed that the woman who no longer needs to be conquered has lost the possessiveness that is vital to love. Priscilla's willingness bordered on apathy.

The void that Priscilla had left, Alec unconsciously filled with affection for his son. There was nothing about Alexander that he would change, not even the infrequent moods of concentration on something indefinable which sometimes momentarily separated them. By mutual understanding they seldom discussed abstract truths and never intimate emotions, but they were otherwise congenial and preferred each other's company to others.

Alec saw to it that Alexander had a firm seat in the saddle, a true eye for shooting and a graceful leg for the ballroom. He cautioned him against obvious egotism and against masturbation, by neither of which Alexander was greatly tempted, and let the other virtues take care of themselves. The sport of the pit and wagering on the race heats, evoked little enthusiasm from either father or son, and they frequented the cockmain and betting posts no more than was essential to their position as men of the world in Mecklenburg.

It troubled Alec a trifle that Alexander saw comparatively little of teen-age companions. But such was the lot of only sons on a plantation. Having survived the same predicament himself, Alec dismissed it from his mind with no serious qualms.

CHAPTER 15

CLOUD OVER CATAWBA

"IF YOU MUST GO to the camp meeting, Priscilla," her husband remonstrated, "of course I'm going with you. It's been fifteen years since you tried one and I think you're in for a disappointment."

"You may be right, Alec, but everyone says the Reverend Peter McClelland is the best preacher in Tennessee."

"Then he should have stayed there. Doesn't he come from those redneck McClellands above your father's place?"

"I knew him as a child," Priscilla said. If Alec had forgotten the later brief crossing of their paths there was nothing to be gained by reminding him. "Pa was interested in him and I believe wrote some friends near his Tennessee lands that he'd make them a good preacher."

"So that's the boy." Alec's memory was better than Priscilla had suspected. "Old Hellfire and Damnation McClelland."

"That's unkind, Alec. He was never that kind of evangelist."

"Well, I don't mind going myself, under the circumstances. But promise me one thing. Leave Alexander at home. I don't want the growth scared out of the boy while he's under six feet."

"As you say, Alec. After you've heard the minister we'll abide by your decision."

"And one more promise. Let's plan to drive back tonight. I'll stay as late as you want if you won't make me sleep in a tent."

Priscilla smiled. "I don't think that is an essential part of the service."

As the camping grounds were only a two hour ride, Alec and Priscilla had an early supper at home. Alexander made less protest at being left than his mother had hoped.

"You're going to be conspicuous in that dress." Alec eyed her reproachfully. Priscilla wore a conservative blue alpaca. "Don't you know the campers outdress the Charlestonians? You'll stand out like a Quaker at a gypsy carnival."

"Why must you tease me, Alec? I'm sure our friends won't wear party clothes to church."

"You won't see many of our friends. These will be mostly Baptists and Methodists."

"Mr. McClelland is a Presbyterian."

"Yes, but from Tennessee. We're growing cold in Carolina."

It was getting dark when the McIntosh carriage rolled in sight of the camping ground grove. Fires could be seen through the trees and women cleaning wooden and iron utensils. Most of the men were lying on the ground smoking, with children of all ages chasing each other and laughing or crying as they succeeded or failed in the competition. The grove was studded with tents of hides or blankets, cabins improvised from materials available and heavy covered wagons with their horses tethered nearby.

In the center of the grove was the high stand for the ministers, several of whom could occupy it at one time. As yet it was vacant but the people were beginning to congregate around it.

Alec and Priscilla got out of the carriage and Pluto was

instructed to drive a quarter of a mile to a farmer's house and unhitch the horses. He was to meet them at the end of the services. To safeguard the Negro from apprehension by the slave patrol, Alec wrote out for him an overnight pass.

On looking about, Priscilla saw only Susan Knox of Unity from her circle of Sunday-meeting friends. The majority of the people were unknown to her. They apparently had ridden many miles and were settled in the woods for the week. Alec had been right about the ladies' regalia. Unlike staid Hopewell, the worshippers assembled in gaudy raiment of the colors of Joseph's coat. Eardrops, beads and rings flashed with every female gesture. Instead of the reverential hush which greeted the Reverend John Williamson's entrance, the multitude continued to chat and laugh gaily as a figure, unfamiliar to Priscilla, mounted the stand.

He announced a hymn, lined the words precisely, then sang them over in a high-pitched key. It sounded a good deal like the spirituals of the slaves. Immediately the audience took up the refrain and the woods reverberated.

This day my soul has caught on fire, *Hallelujah!*
I feel that heaven is coming nigher
O glory Hallelujah!

Alec and Priscilla had brought cushions from the carriage. They placed them on a brushpile a few yards from a deserted fire which continued to burn slowly during the service.

"If you knew how unsuitable the ground is to your ladyship," Alec whispered, "and how unsitable to your lordship you'd have brought chairs instead of pillows."

"I'm very comfortable," Priscilla said, looking like a lost child braving out her bewilderment. She was staring hard at the preachers' stand.

"Is that McClelland?"

"I don't think so," she replied.

The preacher began reading from Matthew, the 24th chapter, the 27th verse:

> For as the lightning cometh out of the east, and shineth even unto the west; so shall also the coming of the Son of man be.
>
> For wheresoever the carcase is, there will the eagles be gathered together.
>
> Immediately after the tribulation of those days shall the sun be darkened, and the moon shall not give her light, and the stars shall fall from heaven, and the powers of the heavens shall be shaken.

"Friends, are you ready? No man knoweth the day or the hour. What secret sins do you harbor? What torments of conscience gnaw at your vitals?"

He continued in the same vein for some twenty or thirty minutes, repeating the same phrases with an intonation resembling the sing-song recitation of poetry.

Priscilla felt herself pulled between an inclination to flee the sensationalism and a fascination at the preacher's hypnotic appeal. Alec's head had dropped on his chest. At peace with the world, the flesh and the devil he breathed rhythmically.

Without warning the evangelist stopped. The silence was so sudden that Alec awoke with a start.

"What's the matter?" he whispered. "Is it over?"

"No, another minister is beginning." An involuntary tremor agitated Priscilla as she recognized the once familiar form of Peter McClelland walking erectly across the stand. By the fitful blaze of the camp fires she could see that his face was lined with furrows. But there was in his expression a glow of peace and serenity he had not possessed as a youth. With a patriarchal dignity he strode across the platform and raised his hands.

Directly beneath the stand was an enclosure referred to as the altar. The evangelist's hands descended and stretched invitingly toward the enclosure. A deep, resonant voice which gave the impression of repressed power broke the hush.

"Here it is, my brothers and sisters. On it was shed the blood of the Lamb. Come."

A woman's hysterical scream echoed through the trees. The Reverend Mr. McClelland repeated his invitation, his voice was charged with emotion but perfectly controlled. Within a matter of minutes, throngs were pushing and shoving toward the altar. Women brought their babes in arms and young men aided their grandsires. Several spirituals were begun at once and the singing and shouting were not always distinguishable.

Around the edge of the circle a group of Negroes had pressed in. Three or four half drunk white men, who had come for no good purpose, were urging the blacks to get the "jerks" and offering them liquor. The Negroes were torn between their terror of the Judgment and the tormenting of the white bullies. If they surrendered to their emotions and fell to the ground, as the example was being set them, the ruffians would burn their feet with brands from the fires.

There were now three ministers on the stand, each exhorting the groups nearest to them. At the altar men and women were singing in exaltation.

When Christians pray, the Devil runs, *Hallelujah!*
And leaves the field to Zion's sons.
O glory Hallelujah.

Above the tumult could be heard the entreaties of the ministers, repeating the theme of the first speaker.

"The sun shall be darkened."

"The moon shall not give her light."

"The stars shall fall from heaven."

"Judgment cometh. Come. Come. Come."

The voice of Peter McClelland, although hardly above bass in register, transcended all others. Its restrained force bore down the tearful pleading of the other two preachers. While his colleagues implored, McClelland commanded.

Groans of sinners writhing on the ground under conviction of guilt could be heard amidst the shouts of those who conceived themselves saved. One band of the latter had formed a line and were marching to their own music imploring their friends as they passed to join them.

About those who lay on the ground, friends and relatives congregated. Some were rubbing their rigid limbs, others trying to raise them to their feet. From the victims came only mad babblings.

Priscilla covered her face with her small hands and burst into tears. Alec had been standing, his arms folded across his chest. A slight flush darkened his face. Without a word he lifted his wife from the ground and carried her to the coach. Pluto he knew by now was deep in the revival. Fastening the horses between the shafts, he drove them home himself.

C H A P T E R 16

AN UNSEASONABLE SPELL of warm weather followed the first frosts of November.

"It must be the effects of the camp meeting," Alec told his wife as they packed his chest for Charleston. "If it's this hot in the Low-country I won't stay long enough to sell much cotton."

"The meeting is over tomorrow," Priscilla remarked. There had been no discussion of further participation by either, and the initial venture had been referred to only briefly by Alec's observation that he now understood Colonel Brevard's solicitude in getting the Reverend Mr. McClelland to Tennessee.

The revival recurred in Priscilla's thoughts with mixed emotions. Peter McClelland had left a lasting impression. It was not his fault, she believed, if the worshippers did not react to his preaching as would a congregation at Hopewell. He spoke more simply than Mr. Williamson, who often attempted the sublime, and he spoke to the heart.

Perhaps Alec should have sent him a message to stop and dine with them. Knowing her husband's prejudices, however, she had not suggested it. The minister had undoubtedly failed to identify them in the crowds, but a woman whom Priscilla believed to be one of his sisters had given her a cold nod of recognition.

"I'll be glad when this year is behind us," Alec continued. "It's been out of kilter ever since it began. We start off on the verge of war for South Carolina's nullification of the tariff, we listen to New England abolitionists denounce us for doing legally to blacks what they do illegally to whites, we read about people flying in balloons over New York and we end up with a rash of revivals. I'll be surprised if we get off without more disruption. It's in the air."

"Something seems to be," agreed Priscilla, fanning herself as she laid a pair of pantaloons in Alec's chest. "I do hope you won't suffer from the heat in Charleston."

"That worries me less," he observed, "than leaving you here. I'm going to stop by Rural Hill on my way and see if some of the girls will come up and stay with you."

"I'd love to have them," replied Priscilla who was more dependent on company than she admitted to herself, "but now that Alexander is beginning to shave I feel that I have a man in the house. And Mr. Riley couldn't sleep very soundly with his wife ailing again."

"You'll be well protected," Alec assured her, "but I'm afraid you'll be lonely with Alexander at school."

Alexander's classes with Mr. Williamson kept him from home the greater part of the mornings. In the back of Alec's mind the recollection that the camp meeting would be breaking up the day of his departure made him uneasy. Priscilla's Price was a good distance from the highway but the overwrought campers might seek a hospitality ordinarily above their claims.

As he rode southward the following morning, he passed several groups in a state of hilarity or moroseness that boded no good for their discretion. He was disappointed at Rural Hill. Priscilla's unmarried cousins who lived at home had crossed the River for a wedding in Lincoln.

The possibility of meeting friends headed for the crossing at Beattie's Ford encouraged him. Whoever they might be he determined to offer them at least a night's lodgings until the campers passed on. Fortune seemed to favor him as he recognized the wagon of Susan Knox and her husband headed for Unity. The other two passengers looked unfamiliar but if friends of the Knoxes they should be acceptable.

He hailed the Negro driver and got out to speak. To his surprise the Knoxes' guests were the Reverend Peter McClelland and his sister Melissa. Alec's intentions underwent a rapid mental review. Preachers, although of a different stripe, had been frequent house-guests at Priscilla's Price. McClelland was doubtless a fanatic but probably harmless with his feet on the ground. Ten miles earlier in the day Alec might have been more circumspect in regard to his wife's protectors. But at Rural Hill he had remained for a stirrup cup and the day was wearing on.

"I will take it as a great favor," he urged, "if you can find it convenient to spend the night at my home. My wife is alone except for our son and the roads, as you know," he hesitated for diplomatic terms, "are full of strangers."

Put on such a basis the invitation could not be declined, and Alec continued on his way with a feeling of relief if not entire satisfaction.

Priscilla found Susan Knox a more agreeable companion than she had been when their school day ambitions had followed divergent paths. With the Reverend Peter McClelland under her roof she experienced an odd sense of gratification. A man of God and a former suitor, or was the latter a conceit of her imaginings? The depths of his attachment he had never revealed, but woman that she was Priscilla had more than a misty remembrance of his flattering confusion in her presence. None of that, of course, mattered now and she assured herself that if more than admiration had moved him it had now passed from his mind. It was singular, nevertheless, that he was still unwed.

Susan's husband, an elder in Unity Church and a respected small farmer, was loquacious company. It was he that Priscilla relied upon to ease the tautness of Peter's sister. Melissa received every overture of hospitality with suspicion. They sat upon the veranda after a supper during which the farmer had held the floor almost without interruption. He continued his observations on things in general and just now the weather in particular.

"Now I've seen a heap of weather in my time, but in all my days I ain't seen nothing to beat that sky."

The others looked politely out and upward, and to their amazement found themselves in full agreement with the speaker. On leaving the lighted hall they had not at first observed the peculiar luster of the atmosphere, but it had now assumed a glittering brilliance that was almost alarming.

"I've studied up some on science," continued the speaker, "have to, you know, to be a good farmer, and I was telling Susan a day or two ago that something was going to come of this heat. All that stuff the frost killed has rotted too quick. The miasma's going to make electricity I'll bet you. It's got to do it to clear the air. Nature's got a way of looking after us, or I reckon, in a manner of speaking, it's God. Ain't that so, Reverend?"

Peter said he felt sure that God knew where every bolt of lightning struck.

"Do you reckon the sun blacking out like a storm will bring on the Judgment?" his sister spoke up. "Sounded like that from the Bible as was read to us. And how about them stars falling down?"

"It was not my understanding," her brother replied, "that these were the causes but the manifestations of the Last Day."

Three or four bright stars shot brilliantly across the heavens.

"Lord, look at that!" shouted Melissa standing up abruptly.

"We frequently see them on this hill," Priscilla attempted to reassure her. "Although I don't remember having seen so many at one time before."

The weirdly glimmering twilight obscured many constellations usually visible, but other falling meteors followed the first group observed.

As night closed down the streaks of light continued to increase and caused the interruption of several of Susan's husband's more lengthy anecdotes.

"The stars in their courses fought against Sisera," quoted the Reverend Mr. McClelland. "This is a beautiful evidence of God's power and care."

About nine o'clock the company broke up for retirement. Priscilla had directed Urania to sweep and air the gate lodge which was used for guests overflowing the mansion house. Urania was further available for any washing the ladies might need after their week's camping, but Melissa declined with small thanks.

"I'll do my own," she told Susan. "I don't want no nigger messin' with my stuff."

Priscilla saw to it that a large ewer of hot water was provided for her from the kitchen fire. Within the last month the inconvenience of pine torches or tinder boxes for lighting candles had been obviated by "Lucifer" friction matches sent up from Charleston. No invention in Priscilla's recollection had resolved so many domestic perils.

CHAPTER 17

PETER MCCLELLAND closed the door of his chamber and sank heavily into a chair. The strain of the last few hours had increased with the passing of the evening. He had spoken directly to Priscilla only when she complimented him on his revival sermon and inquired about his work across the mountains.

"It seems to me," she had said, "that too many of those to whom we look for guidance have deserted us for Tennessee."

She was putting him in the class with Senator Hugh Lawson White and President Jackson. With respect to his own removal, Priscilla had provided more impetus than the needs and opportunities of the frontier, but for a decade and a half the secret had been hid in his heart. The impact of their reunion had pitilessly seared the protective layers of time. Without a warning spark, the smoldering flames flared hotly through him.

By a profane mutation, Peter's spiritual intensity became a naked hunger for Priscilla. There was no disguising the fact from himself. The evangelist was profoundly disturbed. Completely beyond his control, his physical desires dominated his sentient being. The years had served only to enhance those attributes of gentility which had placed the girl on so high a pinnacle above him. In the woman there was now apparent a searching for the things of the soul which the girl had lacked. He could conceive of no culmination of development approaching nearer to perfection in womankind.

Peter took his Bible from his small trunk.

"Heavy is thy rod upon me, O God, but heavier is my sin." Sweat stood out on the back of his hands as he pulled open the glued cloth above the backstrip. He shook the Bible gently toward the floor. At his feet a small blue object rolled once and fixed its light accusingly upon him.

He turned his face away. "Blot out mine iniquity, O God. Against Thee and Thee only have I sinned. The lust of the flesh hath remained within me and I knew it not. Purge me, wash me. O God, help me!"

He did not rise from his chair but sat with his eyes closed and his head upon his clasped hands. For several hours his posture retained its rigidity. In his exhaustion he dozed fitfully and woke himself to continue his wrestling with the tempter. The eerie brightness of the night flooded his room.

Peter's eye caught the reflection of the blue earring on the floor. His vision of eternity was blinded by the pale light. How did he know Priscilla had never yearned for him? A certain rich man had swept her away, any rich man might have done. No choice had been given her to choose between him and another. What a sluggard he had been to give her up. If for one man God made one woman, Priscilla had been made for him.

He struck a Lucifer to catch the time. It was a quarter of twelve. What were Priscilla's thoughts at this moment? Was she, too, awake and pouring out her soul to God as he? If she suffered he must go to her. He must comfort her, pray with her and soothe her troubled breast.

"My God, my God, why hast Thou forsaken me!" Peter cried in bitterness as he sensed the double implication of his thoughts. "Smite me, O God, before it is too late. Give me a sign or pour down Thy judgment upon me."

He opened the door to the yard. Where his feet were bound he dared not think. He stumbled blindly out and stopped.

The stars were falling from the heavens.

"I am mad," he muttered and rubbed his hands across his forehead. With a jerk he pulled his hands to his side and threw back his head to supplicate his God.

The stars continued to fall.

From the slave quarters cries of terror broke into the night. From the kennels came a chorus of uncanine howls. Cocks crew crazily. The seed of Bashan bellowed for home.

The yellow light of a candle silhouetted Priscilla in her bedroom window. Peter stood staring in indecision. Before impulse motivated his feet, the other occupants of the lodge were out in the yard.

"It's the Judgment," screamed Melissa. "Pray, Peter, for God's sake pray!"

Susan Knox got down on her knees. For once her husband failed of enlightening observations. He was as mute as his wife.

"I must go to Priscilla," said Peter and started toward the house.

"You're daft!" His sister laughed hysterically. "Mrs. McIntosh don' first-name you. And she's got her own God."

With an effort Peter restrained his hand from striking his sister's mouth. Instead he clenched his fists tightly by his side. Susan and her husband were oblivious to all but the sky above them. The meteors dropped like fiery snow and left their blazing wakes behind. The red streaks faded into luminous white lines and slowly passed into the night.

Priscilla and Alexander had reached the veranda with their candles. Alexander had neglected his holder and shade and held the taper, spellbound, until the hot wax burnt his fingers. At his side Scipio clutched his arm and jabbered incoherently. For some months past Cornelia had insisted that her son address Alexander as "Youn' Massa" but Scipio usually forgot.

"Fore God, Youn' Massa, it's Judgmen'. Youse gwine take me wid you, ain't you? You gotter hab a nigger to wait on you. I ain't gonner leabe you, Youn' Massa."

The other Negroes pushed in on Priscilla until she was unable to move. They asked questions without waiting for answers. Had time been allowed she would have had none. Beseechingly she looked toward Peter McClelland.

A resonant confident voice arose above the tumult.

"Let us pray."

The Negroes quieted instantly. The dogs ceased howling and fawned towards him, scraping their bellies on the ground.

Through Peter surged the assurance that was his at the height of the camp meeting fervor. His prayer was a supplication for mercy at the second coming of the Lord. That that day was upon them, the Negroes had no doubt. The shower of fire increased in intensity while he spoke. A mellow light bathed the hilltop and the magnificent display radiated from the zenith. Before reaching the horizon, the fireheads faded abruptly but left their ghastly streaks of light.

At the conclusion of the prayer, the Negroes began again to moan. The minister bade them seat themselves in a circle around him as was customary at the camp grounds. In a low voice he began a revival hymn familiar to both

whites and blacks. At the end of the singing he preached
to them from his text at the revival.

Immediately after the tribulation of those days
shall the sun be darkened, and the moon shall not
give her light, and the stars shall fall from heaven
and the powers of the heavens shall be shaken.

Susan Knox, her husband and Melissa McClelland had
moved to the veranda and sat with Priscilla and Alexander on the steps. With his arm around his mother Alexander
remained very quiet. Riley and his family soon joined them.
All listened intently to the minister's words. Priscilla's
misgivings of conscience melted under the warmth of
Peter's voice. "How wonderful," she thought, "to be as
close to God as he."

The sublime spectacle continued throughout the night.
With alternate prayers, exhortations and spirituals, Peter
stilled the panic that threatened them. Fleeing wagons
from nearby farms and plantations joined the McIntosh
circle and found security and peace. At four o'clock the
meteors ran riot in the sky. But aside from the occasional
"Hallelujah!" of an ancient crone there was no disorder.
By daybreak, the fire began to fade.

Riley, with Priscilla's assent, told the slaves there would
be no work until noon if they went quietly to bed.

Anxious about the effects of the night on their own
families, the Unity party did not remain for rest but pushed
on immediately to cross the River. Peter gave Priscilla his
benediction as a man of God. The man of flesh was
conquered.

Alone in her bed with the curtains drawn, Priscilla began
to be afraid. There was no longer a minister under her
roof. How close to Judgment had she come and how far

from preparation was her soul? The worldly triumphs of
her girlhood paraded relentlessly through her mind. Had
God forgiven her these sins? Was this rain of fire a sign of
His displeasure? What a mockery of security was Priscilla's
Price on such a night.

She dreaded the inevitable levity with which Alec would
treat the miracle. Poor Alec, how comfortless his cold philosophy when the face of God appeared. How warm, in
contrast the benediction of the Reverend Peter McClelland:

> The Lord bless thee, and keep thee; the Lord
> make his face to shine upon thee, and be gracious
> unto thee; the Lord lift up his countenance upon
> thee, and give thee peace.

"Miss 'Scilla?" Priscilla heard Urania's voice and pulled
back the curtains.

"I wanna gib you dis here fore you think I stole hit. I
find hit on de floo when I clean up dat Reveren's room."

She handed her mistress a blue bauble, an earring of a
fashion outmoded for fifteen years.

CHAPTER 18

CLOUD OVER CATAWBA

THE PASSING OF the years did not diminish Priscilla's memory of the November night in '33. Whatever the significance of the earring she forced it to an unfrequented corner of her consciousness. A snare and a delusion it might easily become. By far more important for her life was the night's miraculous display of the power of God. Of this she was convinced and on it she meditated often with uncertain forebodings. What did it portend? There was no consolation in opening her soul to Alec. He could not understand if he would. To him the falling stars were merely an astronomical accident. He wrote and thanked the Reverend Mr. McClelland for the protection he had afforded Mrs. McIntosh during the "superstitious panic." Then he forgot the entire episode. Life at Priscilla's Price flowed back into its agrarian social channels.

It was Alec's custom, during cotton growing weather, to take his family to the Catawba Springs. The Springs were the closest approach to a spa the Carolinas afforded and Priscilla had no relish remaining for the fancier fare of the White Sulphur. Alec exerted himself to promote the popularity of the local resort.

"The mineral waters of Lincoln County," he wrote to one of the Lattas who continued to frequent the Virginia Springs, "were analyzed by Professor Olmstead of Chapel Hill, now of Yale, and confirmed to be all that is claimed for them."

With heat vapors as an excuse for those who needed one, the planters of Georgia, Alabama and Low-country South Carolina flocked to western Carolina. Many of the last preferred the higher altitudes of Flat Rock and Fletcher, but on the porches of Catawba Springs, Sinklers, Deas and Hugers from Charleston learned to know Polks, Lockes and Caldwells of the Piedmont.

To refugees from tropical heat the refreshing night coolness was a balm. To the Piedmontese the polite society and salubrious waters were the attractions. Situated on the Great Eastern and Western Line of Stages the resort provided a broadening social influence which the Scotch-Irish of Charlotte and Germans of Lincolnton rarely experienced.

For large planters like the Brevards, Grahams and Alexanders, the Springs provided chiefly a brief respite from plantation routines. In spite of Alec and Major Rufus Reid, who had sold his late father's interest in the Springs but continued an ardent advocate, many continued to travel northward for extensive vacations.

"You have to move away," Alec observed, "to appreciate what you had. We've got more Phifers and Forneys from Alabama here than from Cabarrus and Lincoln. And more Lattas and Springs' from South Carolina than from Mecklenburg."

Mr. Mittag, the portrait painter from South Carolina, found business brisk. Professor Elisha Mitchell of Chapel Hill made the Springs a stopping place for his mountain explorations westward. Not even the Presbyterian ministers, many of whom operated sizable plantations on the side, could resist the healing pools so providentially close at hand. All members of the McIntosh household discovered a level of congeniality.

During one of these pleasant water cures Alexander called his father's attention to a large, bald headed man with piercing eyes.

"That gentleman must have been a soldier, Father," Alexander remarked. "See that scar on his face?"

"Evidently a sabre stroke," Alec observed.

The object of their attention was entertaining a group of fashionable guests on the gallery. His powerful voice boomed out heartily.

"He seems to be quite a social lion," Alec told Priscilla.

"Poor man," she sighed. "He has suffered the smallpox, I see." To herself she thought, "I wonder what he did to deserve the affliction?"

Alec turned to Maxwell Chambers who sat near them. "Have you made the acquaintance of the martial looking gentleman?"

"I have the honor," Mr. Chambers replied. "He is well known in Rowan. He goes by the name of Peter Stewart Ney."

"Oh, I've heard of him," said Priscilla. "Aren't there rumors that he is a French Prince who fought for Napoleon?"

Mr. Chambers hesitated. "It is said he denies it. Whatever his former profession he is now employed as tutor for the older boys. And he not only teaches them, he controls them."

Alec was immediately interested. "A distinguished looking character for a tutor," he remarked. "A good disciplinarian is as rare as a good pedagogue."

"In Mr. Ney you have the exception," Chambers agreed. "And in my opinion the present generation is in sad need of authority. I may someday endow an institution which can control its students. Mr. Ney is also, I am told, a competent, if not exceptional, master of Latin and Greek."

"He should be an expert in French," Priscilla ventured.

"I understand that it pains him to speak it," said Mr. Chambers, "but your boy will learn a great deal of French history if you're planning to engage Mr. Ney. And also some very finished fencing. The old man can knock the foils from the hands of any youngster who challenges him."

"He's worth looking into," Alec commented.

"Is he a religious man, Mr. Chambers?" Priscilla asked anxiously. "So many of the French are infected with infidelity."

"Of his orthodoxy, madame," Chambers answered, "I am hardly a competent judge." The speaker was not an ardent church goer.

"We'll be very sure," Alec stated emphatically, "that no man who tutors Alexander shall undermine his morals."

The statement satisfied Priscilla, and if Maxwell Chambers was aware of any question begging he did not comment upon it.

"Mr. Hampton," Alec continued, "knows the qualifications of all his guests. I'll speak to him this evening."

"I hope," said Priscilla, remembering Mr. Calwell at the White Sulphur, "that his judgments are based on more than worldly distinctions."

That night after supper Alec took the hotel proprietor aside.

"I'm much interested in this Mr. Ney. Can you give me a character?"

"Without qualification," Mr. Hampton replied. "But I know nothing of his antecedents. You can read here in the register what he chooses to disclose."

In the column allotted to the home addresses of hotel

guests, Alec read opposite the signature of P. S. Ney: "An atom floating on the atmosphere of chance."

"Apparently the Frenchman relishes a little mystery," Alec was amused. "However, I'm not concerned with his past. How is he regarded by your acquaintances?"

"There's no question of his integrity," the Proprietor assured him. "I can say unreservedly that Mr. Ney is a high-toned gentleman, far in advance of most in his present profession."

"My wife will be interested in his religion," Alec continued. "Are you acquainted with his sentiments?"

"According to my observations," Mr. Hampton emphasized the last word, "I believe that I could state that his convictions in that realm closely approximate your own and those of Mr. Chambers, with whom I see you are acquainted. He is not a profane man and his morals are unimpeachable."

The Proprietor hesitated a moment.

"I am thinking of asking him," said Alec, "to live in my home."

"Then," Mr. Hampton resumed, "I should add that he does not hold entirely with the recent innovation of our ministers that theology and total abstinence are congential bed-fellows."

"Nor do I," Alec said without much humor. "If he isn't intemperate and doesn't insist on airing his skepticism, I think he is the man I am looking for."

"You need entertain no concern," replied Mr. Hampton, "on either count. Mrs. McIntosh will find him a considerate house-guest. Most of the ladies admire his poetry exceedingly. Some he composes in a religious vein and I am confident he would take pleasure in reading that to your family."

It was not difficult to meet Mr. Ney, and Alec engaged him in several colloquies on the hotel gallery. This, indeed, was the principal diurnal diversion of most of the male contingent present, though an occasional fox hunt was indulged in by the younger spirits.

The old soldier had a dignity that commanded respect. He was not ostentatious in his learning but showed no trace of obsequiousness to slave-baron or senator. The better acquainted Alec became with him the more he was convinced that here were the influences he had sought for Alexander's youth.

After permitting Mr. Ney to out-maneuver him in several lengthy games of chess, Alec presented the proposition for Alexander's education. Mr. Ney was nothing loath to live at Priscilla's Price and stipulated only that he be permitted to tutor several other paying scholars simultaneously and two of his own choosing for charity.

Terms were amicably agreed upon.

Before the services of Mr. Ney were secured, Alexander had received desultory tutoring by between-term students from Chapel Hill and had attended a session or two at Hopewell Academy under the Reverend John Williamson. The minister conducted a respectable school, but Alec had been often depressed by the labored eloquence of Mr. Williamson and preferred for his son less piety and more emphasis on his own precepts for a rewarding life.

Priscilla had no reason to doubt Mr. Ney's conformity to the faith. His strongest oath was "By the Powers!" and his example to his pupils unexceptionable. Alec laughed a little at his excessive use of Eau de Cologne, but to

Priscilla some eccentricities should be condoned in the author of such poems as those he read in her hearing.

Many a restful evening was spent beneath the great portico of Priscilla's Price, with the old preceptor alternately playing the flute and reciting poetry.

"I think I like best," Priscilla suggested, "the verse beginning 'Why should our anxious thoughts extend.' Will you repeat it?"

Mr. Ney obligingly complied.

> Why should our anxious thoughts extend
>   Beyond the prudent cares of life
> Except to that important end
>   Which terminates our mortal strife?
> Nor wealth nor fame will then avail
> To steer our bark or trim our sail.

"And the next verse, too," Priscilla requested.

> Within the span which Heaven prescribes
>   Let all your wishes be confined;
> He who in Providence confides
>   Is happy, cheerful and resigned;
> With manliness his part performs
> In darkness, sunshine and in storms.

"That's mighty fine," Alec declared. He allowed a respectful silence to elapse. "But my favorite, I'm afraid, will always be 'The Cabbage Parboiled.'"

> Best of the garden, why should we
> Withhold a stanza due to thee?
> Roses may entertain the eye
>   And gratify the smell:
> With cabbage and good bacon I
>   Can hunger's tooth repel

Pride of the kitchen, why should we
Withhold the praises due to thee?
Let emblematic flowers imply
    Emotions tongues cannot explain;
Good cabbages well cook'd defy
    Keen appetites, and life sustain.
Boast of the dinner table, we
Award these praises due to thee
We could give thee a sweeter name,
But still thy virtues are the same.

Late one evening, when Priscilla and Alexander had retired, Alec and his house-guest began a congenial discussion of the philosophy of Tom Paine's *Age of Reason*. A pitcher of rum toddy served to loosen their tongues. It was not long before Mr. Ney had brought the conversation around to his favorite topic, Napoleon's campaigns. Alec knew little French history, but found the old gentleman an entertaining raconteur.

"Much of great importance has never been recorded," Mr. Ney observed. "And much that has been written is inaccurate. The recent *History of Napoleon* by Laurent de l'Ardeche is a case in point. I have only turned the leaves but found many errors. As for the portrait of Marshal Ney, I could draw a better myself."

Alec gave him a questioning look.

Mr. Ney hesitated, then finished off his glass.

"I think I can confide in you, Mr. McIntosh," he said solemnly. "The reports concerning my identity are not fabrications. I was . . . . "

He straightened up in his chair.

"I am . . . Marshal Ney of France!"

The confidence did not take Alec entirely off guard.

The claim was often made by Mr. Ney's admirers. With no indication of surprise, Alec raised his drink respectfully.

"Your health, Sir," he said.

The aged veteran then put his hand in turn upon his many scars of battle. For each he recalled with relish the campaign or encounter in which it was won. The role of "the bravest of the brave" was not glossed over. He followed this with an account of his mock execution, the red fluid, the disguise, and the smuggling aboard ship for America.

"If anyone presumes to think that my own men," he concluded excitedly, "would fire on Marshal Ney, he does not know the French grenadier!"

Alec was fascinated by the story. It was common knowledge but no one told it beter than the chief protagonist himself. If Alec retained his incredulity, his countenance did not betray it.

"The old tutor," he thought to himself, "is further in his cups than his elocution indicates. He'll forget by tomorrow."

Mr. Ney read his mind. "*In vino veritas*," he declared with unsteady dignity.

The subject was never mentioned between the two again.

CHAPTER 19

In SPITE of his classical course with the Reverend Samuel C. Caldwell, Alec never read Greek and Latin for pleasure. The library of Priscilla's Price contained the classic authors in hand-tooled but rarely opened volumes. Shakespeare, Samuel Johnson and Lord Chesterfield came from the Brevards. Alex had purchased the popular poets: Byron, Burns, Scott and Moore, in decorative cabinet editions. And Priscilla owned the works in quarto of Calvin, Knox, Witherspoon and Archibald Alexander. It was a respectable but not a distinguished collection.

Peter Ney opened a new vein of interest for Alec.

"I perceive," observed the Tutor, "that you would foster in Alexander a love of his country, or more specifically, an affection for the Piedmont. A praise-worthy aim it is. Few men contribute to the future who have no feeling of obligation to the past."

Alec agreed, though his own ambitions for the future did not extend greatly beyond the banks of his native Catawba.

"If your son is to cherish his heritage," Mr. Ney continued, "he must understand it. For that a library of local literature is essential."

"Local literature?" asked Alec puzzled. "There isn't enough to fill a shelf, much less a library."

"I beg to differ," returned the Tutor. "It is available but uncollected. If you approve the project I believe I can convince you."

"Well, you set up the program," Alec agreed. "I'll pay the

bills and to Alexander, I trust, will go the profit."

"First," Mr. Ney suggested, "you must have a bookplate." The old teacher had a gift for sketching. He drew rapidly a flowing river, which might have been the Catawba, and above it a single cloud.

Alec looked on, interested. "Why the cloud?" he asked. "Is it protecting or threatening?"

"As you choose to regard it," said Ney enigmatically. "I'll give you my interpretation of the rest of it. The river represents the perpetuation of the McIntosh line, its rapidly flowing current a purification from unworthiness. The regional significance, aside from the symbolism, is apparent."

Being unaccustomed to a personal application of art, Alec was much intrigued. On his next trip to Philadelphia, he had the sketch engraved over the legend "Ex Libris Alexander McIntosh Junior." The imprint of the river had a quality of timelessness. As for the cloud, like Mr. Ney's past, it remained a mystery.

"If Priscilla Price were in either South Carolina or Virginia," Alec told his librarian, "there'd be plenty to fill our shelves. North Carolina has been asleep so long the journals are beginning to refer to us as 'Old Rip'. "

"In printing," Mr. Ney replied, "it's true that this state has lagged behind. But we are not devoid of *literati*. Both Dr. Hugh Williamson and Judge Francois Xavier Martin have written histories of Old North."

"But neither man," Alec returned, "was a native born Tar-Heel."

"Nor for that matter," said Ney, "was either opus published in the State. Both facts, in my opinion, are of secondary importance. The cultural significance of the books rests in the subject matter and the residence of the authors within our bounds."

"From that point of view," Alec observed, "General Joseph Graham was the most valuable citizen on the River, although his recollections were only printed in the *Catawba Journal*."

"They will undoubtedly be republished," Mr. Ney predicted. "Regardless of inaccuracies in detail, as must be true of all reminiscenses, they constitute a mine of information concering the Revolution in the Piedmont."

"I don't think he left anything out," Alec laughed. Many a night on the porch of Catawba Forge he had listened to Colonel Brevard and General Graham review the events of the war. At the time, a gig ride with Priscilla had been preferable. He only now began to appreciate the contribution of the veterans.

"You should take your files of the newspapers," advised Mr. Ney, "to William Hunter's shop on West Trade and have them bound. Russian calf will preserve them and is less costly than vellum or morocco."

Alec thought a minute. "I believe I have all the *Catawba Journal* and all the *Miners and Farmers Journal*. I am getting the *Charlotte Journal* now. Since I don't keep a day book they serve for records. Binding will help."

"That gives you all the Charlotte journals," Mr. Ney commented. "I don't suppose you take the *Western Carolinian*, it being a Salisbury paper? To my thinking, it is the best in the west as well as the most successful. We can no doubt purchase copies in Rowan. It belongs in your library."

"Well, I do have most of the Salem almanacs," Alec remembered. "They're out in the office." The farming aids, medicinal remedies, common sense and broad humor of Blum's *Farmers and Planters Almanac* appealed to something in the McIntosh make-up. Alec had thrown none away and nearly twenty issues were found.

"We ought to bind these in morocco," Alec beamed. "They're valuable."

"The volume will be," Mr. Ney agreed. "Someday this may be the only book of its kind in the world."

Alec's voice took on a note of enthusiasm. "I never thought of making your own books."

"What other Piedmont printings have you in the office?" Mr. Ney queried, pleased with his success.

"Oh, a lot of stuff on the Mecklenburg Declaration," Alec replied. "Father was there in '75 and I like to keep up with the controversy. My people were only observers. The Brevards were the literary lights."

"In that subject alone," Mr. Ney said impressively, "you have a unique basis for a local library. Your son's forebears were protagonists whom a grateful nation will come more and more to honor. *Alenda lux ubi orta libertas.* Let learning be cherished where liberty was born."

"Then your faith wasn't shaken by the correspondence of Jefferson and Adams?"

"The letters gave only opinions, not proofs," Ney replied. "It is unfortunate that Mr. Jefferson's observations weren't published when written. He could have been answered."

"I have the reply of Jo Seawell Jones written after Jefferson's death," said Alec. "It's the only book I know on the Declaration. But there are a good many pamphlets and orations. We'll take a look."

On the office shelves was found a copy of the pamphlet

printed by the State in 1822, the first official word from North Carolina on the much mooted subject. Also represented was the second state pamphlet, written in '31 shortly after the Adams-Jefferson correspondence had been made public.

There were several publications issued for the "Grand Celebration" of 1835, amongst them a stylish invitation to an Independence Ball in Charlotte. Alec regarded it ruefully. It had not been accepted. A decade previously such select affairs in Mecklenburg would have rejoiced Priscilla's heart. As it was he had only been able to persuade her to attend the less frivolous events. They had met Governor Swain and Senator Mangum, listened to the address of Franklin L. Smith, and heard the Salem Band play the marches to Generals Polk and Graham and the Mecklenburg Grand March. Alec would have preferred to remain for the toasts (of which there had been over one hundred drunk) but Priscilla was anxious to get Alexander away from the crowds. The publications remained to remind him of his disappointment.

When collected, the pamphlet literature on the Declaration made a neat volume. Alec took a proprietary interest in it. He must persuade Alexander to read it.

In the realm of theology, he found an enthusiastic helpmeet in Priscilla. The published sermons and polemics of the Reverends James Hall, Samuel Eusebius McCorkle, James McRee, James Wallis and Samuel C. Caldwell had been religiously preserved since before Priscilla's birth by Aunt Sally. To these Priscilla added over a dozen from later or lesser pulpit lights, of which the largest number came from Dr. John Makemie Wilson of Rocky River. Alec's vellum volume of *Presbyterian Sermons* was even more impressive than his collection on the Declaration.

"I'm sure the minister's wife we met in Philadelphia," Priscilla suggested, "can find some of the books by the Reverend John Thomson of Center. He and Alexander Craighead may have differed as to interpretation of the Scriptures, but they were both men of God."

"If Mr. Thomson wrote any of his books while at Center," said Alec with an inspiration, "they would be the earliest written in this section."

"A first edition for the Piedmont," exclaimed Mr. Ney, "if the discovery is made. In any event he was your first resident author. The Presbyterian ministers have been the most prolific of your *literati*. It could not be proved, I suppose, that Dr. Alexander MacWhorter wrote any of his published sermons while president of Liberty Hall, but he was bred in this section and spoke its mind better than many who never left it."

"Except for the sermon preached at his funeral," said Alec who had been presented with the slim volume by Aunt Sally, "we're pretty short on biography. Mecklenburg needs a Plutarch."

"There will be lives of your Mecklenburg Signers written," Mr. Ney was confident.

"And I am sure," Priscilla added, "that future generations cannot forget Reverend Alexander Craighead. He was a greater man than many governors."

"The trouble about the statesmen," Alec decided, "is that they have to move away to become famous. Old Hickory has the Catawba River in his blood but he'd never have become President if he'd stayed here."

"It's a rare prophet or poet," opined Mr. Ney, "who is honored at home."

"We have no poets to honor," Alec laughed, and then

checked himself, "with the exception of yourself, of course."

"*Poeta nascitur, non fit,*" observed Mr. Ney, "but including your servant the Piedmont has its homespun bards. The *Western Carolinian* prints verse by many others besides myself. Since most are unsigned I doubt you'll have names to honor but the inspiration is there."

"In my scrapbooks," Priscilla confided, "there are many beautiful sentiments in verse. I clipped several by the Reverend Humphrey Hunter from the *Catawba Journal.*"

"I have heard from the old soldiers," Mr. Ney added, "a number of spirited ballads of the Revolution in this section. If Charlotte were Charleston or Boston, they would have been in the journals. It's a loss that no one has preserved them."

"If we dig any up," Alec suggested, "you can have Alexander memorize them along with his Horace and Virgil. *Arma virumque cano* is as appropriate to the Catawba as to the Tiber. The way Alexander can rattle off the *Shorter Catechism* he must have good memory faculties."

"He has indeed," his tutor commented, "and he may inherited a talent for riming. His great-uncle Adam Brevard's 'Mecklenburg Censor' is a very witty piece."

"For which," Priscilla smiled, "I have always heard Uncle Adam was almost tarred and feathered. I trust Alexander's abilities will take a more dignified turn."

"All of which proves," Mr. Ney concluded, "that the Piedmont is not without its literary tradition. It needs direction and it needs polish, but the impetus is present."

With plenty of time on his hands and the collector's itch urging him on, Alec beset the newspaper presses for copies of obscure and forgotten pamphlets. Though Charlotte had been several decades behind Salisbury and Lincolnton in establishing newspapers she made up for lost time as her anniversary celebrations and educational institutions became established.

Alec found Priscilla's clerical callers his most appreciative collaborators. He was even willing to condone their increasing reluctance to share the contents of his sideboard decanters. Preaching was a poor way to make a living and you couldn't found a family moving around all the time, but Alec admitted that some of the profession were "right clever fellows."

The library at Priscilla's Price soon numbered over a hundred titles of local literature. Bound in volumes by William Hunter of Charlotte or by more expert cratfsmen in Charleston and Philadelphia, they presented an imposing appearance in the handsome Elfe secretary.

In comparison with the number of books belonging to the Mecklenburg Caldwells or the Lincoln County Brevards, the collection was small in content. But for Alexander McIntosh, Jr., there was unique opportunity for understanding the civilization founded by his fathers.

CHAPTER 20

CLOUD OVER CATAWBA

THE QUESTION of sending Alexander to college had been discussed in a desultory fashion. Higher education was by no means essential for respectability or success as a planter.

"If the boy wants to be a lawyer, physician or preacher," observed Alec with the prejudice of his class, "college is all right. But most professions are only good stepping stones for poor boys to a planter's estate." And Alexander was not poor.

In Mr. Ney collegiate advantages found a champion.

"The conception of a university," he told his employer, "as the parent of the learned professions alone is becoming obsolete. In your youth it was the accepted practice of those with means to study with the ministers, whatever their choice of livelihood. Now the sons of these men are going to college. Liberal education should be widely diffused *pro bono publico*."

The truth of this theory had already been recognized by a few Piedmont connections such as the Brevards. Priscilla's uncles had traveled to Princeton before the Revolution. Her brothers and cousins were graduates of the University of South Carolina. Through no fault of the McIntoshes a bachelor's degree had been acquired as a family tradition. Alexander might conform if he chose, but where should he go?

Since the death of President Joseph Caldwell, the University at Chapel Hill had lost much of its appeal to Piedmont Presbyterians. Thomas Jefferson's university at Charlottesville was becoming the fashion for Southern youth, but its reputation for free-thinking in theology was second only to that of South Carolina College under Dr. Thomas Cooper. The latter had recently been forced by parental solicitude to retire. Priscilla was greatly relieved when Alexander showed no interest in the public-supported institutions. The church college at Princeton was too far into abolitionist country for safety. And Alec put down his foot aganist the blue-nosed seminaries of New England.

"We've got enough self-righteousness in Mecklenburg already," he said.

Alexander had made gratifying progress under the tutelage of Mr. Ney. After Mair's *Introduction to Latin Syntax* and *Graeca Minora,* he was ready for Caesar's *Punic Wars* and Xenophon's *Anabasis.* The mathematics text was a long-hand production by Mr. Ney himself. For recreation they read together the English belles-lettres and modern history.

"When our formal association is concluded," advised the tutor, "I hope you will continue to construe your Cicero and Greek Testament. You will then be adequately equipped for any institution in the country."

Alexander followed his advice.

There was no occasion to hurry off to college. Beyond business trips with his father to Philadelphia, Camden, and Charleston and summer vacations at Catawba and Virginia Springs, Alexander had seldom been long from home. He was content with the duties and diversions of Priscilla's Price and was not conscious of the lack of a wider companionship than he had known.

Several years before Mr. Ney took over Alexander's education, Alec had been approached by the Reverend Robert Hall Morrison for a subscription to the new college being established in upper Mecklenburg. Dr. Morrison had married Priscilla's cousin, Mary Graham, and in spite of chronic ill-health (which finally took him off at ninety) had labored heroically in launching the college. The campus was originally a part of the Beaver Dam plantation of William Lee Davidson II, whose wife was an aunt of Mary Morrison and of Priscilla.

At first the institution appeared to Alec as only another minister's classical school of which there had been many in Mecklenburg. But when Dr. Morrison informed him that subscriptions of a thousand or more each had been secured from James G. Torrance, Dr. Winslow Alexander and three of the Davidsons (not all of whom were notably devout), his indifference diminished.

Although the College was controlled by the church presbyteries, it was almost a family undertaking. All the large subscribers, including Dr. Morrison, were connected by marital ties. Clearly the institution would be in the hands of the most substantial men of the Piedmont. When its charter was qualified by a prohibition of religious discrimination, Alec signed up for five hundred dollars.

"I'm giving this," he told Dr. Morrison, "in memory of Priscilla's Aunt Sally who was a better Presbyterian than I ever hope to be."

As a politic move the college was christened "Davidson" in honor of the Revolutionary brigadier. Names implying a denominational connection met with opposition in the legislature and incurred less support from those whose loyalty was remunerative.

"Mecklenburg is a good location for a college," said Alec in conversation with President Morrison. "I hope this one will last longer than Queens. Your manual labor system, however, seems doubtful of success to me."

Dr. Morrison begged to differ. "The connection between the mental and corporeal parts of our frame," he explained, "is so intimate and important that the healthful development of both ought to be prized as a solemn duty."

"A commendable theory," Alec acquiesced, "but your scholars coming from Rural Hill, Mount Mourne, Elmwood and Alexandriana won't take kindly to an 'overseer'. "

"The rich, I fear," Dr. Morrison observed, "will be in the minority. It is unquestionably a work of benevolence to bring the means of an education within the reach of as many of our fellow men as we can dispose and enable to improve them. There is no 'overseer'. The labor will be supervised by a Steward."

But names didn't alter actualities, and Alec was an accurate prophet. The system proved both unsuccessful and unnecessary. President Morrison was soon writing to prospective patrons:

"The great majority of Students here are from the first families of the Community." And of the early commencements his letters stated with satisfaction: "I have never seen any occasion which called together so many of the intelligent, and rich and influential members of society as our Public Examinations."

Many of Mr. Ney's pupils attended Davidson College. The old tutor was a frequent and welcome figure on the hill. He borrowed books from the library and made marginal annotations in those relating to Napoleon. When the trustees voted to adopt a seal for authenticating official documents, they called upon Peter Ney to design it. A sword resembling Napoleon's was drawn transfixing a serpent of ignorance and sin. Around the design Mr. Ney engrossed a motto: *Alenda Lux Ubi Orta Libertas.*

On one of his visits to the campus, Mr. Ney took Alexander as his guest. They secured accommodations for the night at the large brick house operated by Mr. Dinkins. It stood across the public road from the campus and many of the students braved the Red Sea of the muddy Satesville highway to greet their former preceptor. The next day the old gentleman was received as a celebrity by the boys. As Mr. Ney did not consider his reception excessive, Alexander concluded it was genuine and shared his host's ratification.

To Priscilla's intense relief and Alec's quiet satisfaction, Alexander decided to matriculate at Davidson College. He took Scipio with him to cut his wood and attend his horse and found lodgings with acquaintances in one of the small dormitories on Oak Row.

As became the dignity of a collegiate scholar, Alexander wrote formally, if irregularly, to his parents.

Davidson College, N. C.

Honored Parents,

Thanks to Mr. Ney I am not finding the recitations here difficult although I have been assigned to the Junior Class. Some of the students are very poorly prepared and others do not exhibit marked ambition to excel, but I have not yet made the acquaintance of one I do not like.

There are two literary societies here, the Philanthropic and the Eumenean. Most of the North Carolina students join the former and I have accepted their invitation to become a member. We hold our debates in the Chapel which is about midway between the quadrangles. I work harder for Society than I do for classes.

Dr. Morrison calls me "Cousin McIntosh" which is very gracious of him and I like him very much. Professor Sparrow teaches languages. Do you remember the time he preached at Unity and his maternal parent shouted throughout the sermon? Of course, I would not refer to that here. The third professor is Mr. Johnston. He does not appear to be a pedagogue of distinguished parts.

Scipio sends his regards to his mother as I do to my own and Father.

Your obedient son,
Alexander McIntosh, Jr.

Davidson College, N. C.
Honored Parents,

Yours of the 15th ult. received and would have been answered but for the press of business here. Scipio will be the bearer of this and explain more fully his presence at home. Only a very few of the students brought their servants with them and all, I think, have done as I and sent them home. It does not ingratiate a man here to maintain a negro. The students look on you as stuck-up and I would not wish my class mates to think that I entertain a higher opinion of myself than they do. I do not object to drawing my own water and laying my fires. There is a college servant but he seems to be generally employed by the faculty during the hours we could make use of him.

No more at present as this is Saturday night, and I must heat the water for my bath.

Your obedient son,
Alexander McIntosh, Jr.

P.S. Mother will be gratified to learn that I have joined the Students Temperance Society.

Davidson College, N. C.

Honored Parents,

It is with remorse that I note that several weeks have elapsed since my visit home. My fellow students have given me a very flattering testimonial of their regard by electing me to office in Society. I am devoting all my energies to merit so high an enconium.

Father need entertain no alarm that I am undermining my health by burning the mid-night oil. The gentlemen of the faculty inspect our quarters to see that we retire at a respectable hour. From the students the response is not always all that could be wished but their recalcitrancy does not stem from a desire to study. Only a small percentage are members of the Temperance Society. A sophomore from Alabama was recently given the lash for cursing a professor.

Cousin Mary Morrison frequently invites me for supper. She lives in the small brick house at the north end of the campus. According to my last calculation she now has five daughters. I often remain for evening prayers and have had the honor to lead them when Dr. Morrison is preaching from home.

Your obedient son,
Alexander McIntosh, Jr.

Davidson College, N. C.

Honored Parents,

Within a few weeks I shall have the dual

pleasure of becoming a next session senior and being again under your roof. It would be difficult if not impossible to express to you my gratitude for the advantages of this year at College. I am confident that I have already become a different, and I pray God a better, man.

Much has transpired since I last saw you in Charlotte. President Morrison has definitely made up his mind to resign on account of his health. I understand he will build on the plantation Uncle Joseph Graham left Cousin Mary. It is said the Reverend Samuel Williamson will be elevated to the President's chair. I personally admire him even more than I do his brother at Hopewell.

The Manual Labor System has become voluntary and is on its way to extinction. While I do not wish to be the bearer of tales it is doubtless well known that many of the students resented bitterly their subjection to the steward. Wagons were raced from the fields spilling most of their loads before reaching their destination; tools were broken or unaccountably lost; and once a pig was tied to the recess bell to terminate the day's work. For the sake of Dr. Morrison I regret that a system which has proved beneficial to many other institutions should fail so dismally here.

Our days are very full from Morning Prayers before breakfast until Evening Prayers after candle light. Prayers are well attended as attendance is compulsory but I would that a larger number of the Davidson students were genuinely pious. Such is not the case.

Your obedient son,
Alexander McIntosh, Jr.

Davidson College, N. C.

Honored Parents,

In reply to Father's inquiry as to what we do when not occupied with classes or prayers, I will try to give a succinct account of our leisure. Since the Manual Labor System has been abolished we have no set schedule between our closing class and Evening Prayers. The Societies frequently have a contest at alley-cat or shinny. My abilities are better suited to the latter and I may say without self-praise that my Society considers me an asset. I have the honor to serve regularly as goalie.

Dancing, as you know, is contrary to church regulations, and I voluntarily relinquished it on Dr. Morrison's solicitation. There is no objection to secular singing on week days and a number of students have flutes and fiddles. After candle-light there is usually a music party on the stoop of one of the dormitories. Formerly the singing of "Home Sweet Home" or "Rocked in the Cradle of the Deep" affected my sensibilities with an uncontrollable longing for home but I have now become better adjusted to my situation.

The companionship of my contemporaries has become so congenial to my tastes that I do not anticipate the isolation of plantation management with the eagerness I formerly entertained. Mr. Williamson has exhorted with me in private concerning my future estate. He has a wonderful assurance regarding matters of the Spirit.

Your obedient son,
Alexander McIntosh, Jr.

Davidson College, N. C.

Honored Parents,

It appears hardly credible that two years have elapsed since my matriculation at this institution. Whereas formerly living in close proximity with others affected me as an unnatural circumstance, the converse now appears to be the case. With no diminishing of the respect and devotion I entertain for you I discover upon my return here from visits home that I have a natural inclination for the society of a large assemblage. It is not that I would turn any powers of persuasion I may exercise upon others to my own advantage. Rather I would use what talents God has granted me through you to the service of my fellows.

I have been in frequent conference and prayer with President Williamson. He is not so polished as his brother at Hopewell nor as Dr. Morrison but is a zealous counselor in the Faith. By the students he is highly esteemed for his candor. Our Society has commissioned Mr. Mittag to paint his portrait which we trust will one day adorn the walls of our own hall.

It has pleased the faculty to confer upon me the honor of delivering the Latin salutatory next month. I am very sensible of the obligation upon me. I look forward to your presence on that occasion and sincerely hope that it will be in my power, *Dei gratia,* to acquit myself to the satisfaction of the most generous of all parents.

Your obedient son,
Alexander McIntosh, Jr.

CHAPTER 21

CLOUD OVER CATAWBA

THE MCINTOSH CORTEGE included Scipio, whose self respect required redemption after his expulsion from college, and Cornelia, who, if not bone of Alexander's bone could at least claim a share of its marrow. Owing to infirmities, Pluto shared the driving with Scipio and admonished him in the etiquette of coachmanship. Mrs. Brevard's maid found a precarious seat at Cornelia's feet. Her mistress, now a widow, was paying an extensive visit to her daughter. The four Negroes observed the dignified decorum due the occasion. Since Commencement came in August, the seats outside were actually more comfortable than the closed-in plush bottoms occupied by the family.

The coach was en route to the home of Major Rufus Reid, where its occupants would stay while not attending the public exercises. Major Reid's Mount Mourne plantation was only four miles north of the College. Being a son of Captain John Reid of Unity and Catawba Springs and a special crony of Alec's, the Major had been foster "uncle" and frequent host to Alexander during his years at Davidson.

In addition, Major Reid's second wife had been the widow of Mrs. Brevard's brother, a ramification of kinship so comparatively simple amongst Catawba families as to make them almost blood relations. Since the Major's first and second wives had been sisters (and, incidentally, step-aunts of his third), there had been considerable doubt concerning the soundness of his theology. In Fayetteville, a Presbyterian preacher had recently been suspended from his pulpit for marrying his wife's sister. But the Major stood his ground and kept his women.

Mrs. Brevard contended that the elegant Mount Mourne mansionhouse had been built with her sister-in-law's money but she felt compelled to forego any Scriptural and financial scruples respecting its master in order to see her nephews. It was not without aptness, she thought, that the Major himself referred to his home site as "Mount Diable."

The gleaming white mansion radiated a cotton planter's welcome. It was closer to the highway than Priscilla would have placed it, but the elevation was excellent. The handsomest frame house in the Piedmont deserved to be where people could see it. Inside, the folding doors between the southern rooms had been pushed aside and the large apartment was noisy with neighbors invited in to greet the guests.

Priscilla recognized Osborne kin, Emersons, Whites, Stinsons and Houstons. A familiar face was that of old Mrs. Latta, twice the Major's mother-in-law and once his step-grand. She lived across the public road in her own cottage and took care of the offspring lost in the hymeneal intricacies. In the course of the evening Priscilla noticed that Alec and the Major were having uncommon merriment at the expense of the old lady. As a Knox of Unity she could meet the enemy at the gate but Priscilla decided she was unfairly put upon. She went over to defend the distaff platform.

"Sometimes I think you're the devil's own," the ireful saint remarked to her son-in-law. "Did you notice the barn," she turned to Priscilla, "when you drove up?"

Priscilla had not.

"Well, I hope you won't have the opportunity tomorrow," said Mrs. Latta. "After much earnest effort we prevailed on Major Reid to paint a notice there with respect to the forthcoming revival. What he has done is a sacrilege."

On the morrow as the McIntosh coach drove out for Davidson, Priscilla read in large letters on the side of the barn:

Coming Next Week
Three Revivalists
To abuse and vilify the Devil.

The dusty road was crowded with the populace of the countryside. Not even a camp meeting was dearer to the people than a commencement at their college. Pedestrians carried their Sunday shoes, saddle horses bore families on pillions, and the vehicles varied from farm wagons to coaches of every vintage. The appearance of lunch baskets indicated that most intended to make a day of it.

Alexander did not perform until the second day and had leisure on the first for those startling revelations that meeting the parents of one's classmates often bring. Polish, he concluded, had little in common with heredity. The South Carolina families outnumbered all others except the Tar Heels. The Alabamians were next, a large number of Carolinians having lately migrated to that Gulf state. There was no snobbery in Alec, but he was gratified that the associates of his son at college had included many from River plantations comparable to his own. From Lincoln County came representatives of the Mount Tirzah Brevards, the Burton Place Burtons and the Elm Wood Grahams. From Mecklenburg in addition to Alexander's cousins from Rural Hill and Oak Lawn were sons of the Alexanders, Torrances, Caldwells and Springs.

"There is a virtue," Mr. Ney had once advised Alec, "in growing up with companions neither too far above or below your own estate."

There was also a virtue, Alec believed, in having the heir of Priscilla's Price speak the language of those who like himself must draw their sustenance from the Indian river.

The exercises for the day were held in the brick chapel which stood in the center of the college buildings. Dignified with a classic portico of four large columns it was considered an imposing structure by many of the rural inhabitants. Alec was not greatly impressed, although there was no church in the valley of equal pretentions.

"Our Chapel, Father," Alexander pointed out, "is said to be situated on the highest point between the Catawba and the Yadkin Rivers. In rainy weather, Dr. Morrison used to say, the water from the roof to the west drains into the Catawba and that to the east into the Yadkin."

Alec praised the location but thought the commencement hall hardly large enough to accommodate the crowds which continued to gather.

In the afternoon the sophomores and juniors spoke. The McIntosh and Reid parties concluded to relinquish their seats to those with sons on the platform. The August heat was less fatal to stocks and starched petticoats under the oaks of the campus.

After candle light in the evening the Eumenean and Philanthropic Societies held their annual celebrations. On the left lapels of their coats the members wore rosettes of blue or pink ribbons with streamers. Society colors were sported by the students with as much determination as were ever Whig and Democrat cockades by their parents.

Since the honor of the Phi's meant much to Alexander, his parents gave the program their close attention and as warm applause as the weather permitted.

On issuing forth from the speakings, the crowd beheld an illuminated welcome from their hosts. The fronts of the Oak and Elm Row tenements were ablaze with candles. A promenade with sons, brothers and beaux was the closing high-light of the evening. The quadrangle walks were shortly filled with a close-order procession. As the Dinkins House was the only inn of the village, Alec could not but wonder where so many guests would lay their heads. But undoubtedly Wood Lawn, Glenwood and Beaver Dam were as expansive as Mount Diable and the concourse dispersed at an honest hour.

The next morning was sufficient evidence that the College was the favorite of the people be their connection mechanic, merchant, farm producer or patron. Only the 20th of May rivalled a Davidson commencement as the fete day for Mecklenburg. Visitors from a distance were much impressed with the popularity of the infant institution. That Latin and Greek were beyond the ken of the majority did not abate their enthusiasm. In spite of the stifling heat of the small chapel, the young orators acquitted themselves with ardor. When the ten seniors in turn had delivered their parting sentiments, President Williamson followed with the Baccalaureate. The exercises were closed by a benediction from the most venerable minister present.

Neither Alec or Priscilla had been able to follow the purport of Alexander's Latin oration, but its syllables rolled with a good classic ring and it was heartily cheered by the audience. The boy spoke with an evangelical earnestness. To Alec came the unwelcome premonition that his son was headed for holy orders. Priscilla lost much of the happiness she had hoped to share in Alexander's success in a vain effort to conquer her pride in his intellectual prowess.

"Your son," President Williamson told them, "has sustained an unblemished character during his residence with us. There is no member of his class from whom I anticipate greater service to the Master."

"A Christian layman," Alec returned with more force than warmth, "may exert a great influence for good."

Alexander was unusually quiet during the long drive towards the River.

"Parting is hard on the boy," thought Alec with vague uneasiness. "When we get home I'll dig out some ice for a julep. A college graduate is old enough for a drink with his father." He turned the talk to the year's crop of cotton.

"I often wonder," he remarked, "if thinning out every other stalk might not in the long run produce the best bolls. I'll give you the west field next year and you can try it out with Scipio."

Alexander's reply was non-committal. "If you approve it, Father, I'm sure it's a sound experiment."

"Now that you are a bona fide bachelor," Alec tried again, "it might be well for us to decide what part of the plantation you prefer to start with on your own. Have you given it any thought?"

The boy shifted uneasily and took his mother's hand.

"Not yet, Father," he replied.

"Dr. Williamson spoke very highly of you, son," Priscilla remarked.

"I hope I can deserve it," Alexander said seriously, and again relapsed into silence.

When the coach pulled to a halt in front of the shadowy columns of Priscilla's Price, Alexander made no move to get out. His eyes met Alec's with steadiness.

"Father," he said, "I think I should tell you now. I am satisfied after much earnest prayer that I have a call to preach the Gospel."

CHAPTER 22

To ALEC his son's decision was a knell to his hopes for Priscilla's Price.

"If preaching will make Alexander happy," he told Priscilla, "that, of course, is what the boy must do."

But Alec couldn't understand it. For a man of his temperament the obligation he felt to his land and home was sufficient to make a life worth living. The plowing and planting in the spring, the scraping and hoeing during summer, the picking, ginning and baling in the fall and the triumphal progress of the yield of the season to Charleston formed a cycle of unending interest.

Alec's patriarchal relationship to his Negroes, who were now more numerous than the land could profitably employ, satisfied his masculine urge for domination. The plantation required annually more careful husbanding. But it was worth it. The master of Priscilla's Price had a good place under the Piedmont sun.

For a time he felt a flare of resentment against Davidson College for turning his son from the land. But he recognized the injustice of the accusation. Only two men of the forty who had belonged to Alexander's class had elected to become ministers. Unlike the gentlemen of the faculty, the student body was not conspicuously pious. The boy's choice was as fundamentally the influence of his mother at home as of his Alma Mater at college.

To Priscilla, Alexander's decision was a benediction from heaven. That God had called her son to the Gospel ministry filled her soul with gratitude. Alexander was saved from the snare of worldliness and the blight of pride that had broken her life.

"Ministers," Aunt Sally had said, "at least of the Presbyterian denomination, are chosen of the Spirit. They are assured of salvation."

Alexander made no such claims, but his humility was, to his mother, only another indication of his positive election. Her son would make intercession for her at the Throne of Grace. In God's own time she would be eternally united with Alexander and little Sarah.

One doubt remained to impair Priscilla's thanksgiving. As time passed Alec's lukewarm participation in Hopewell observances diminished almost to inactivity. If only he would search his spirit. From his youth up, she knew, he had observed the letter of the sacred law. Yet his life lacked consecration.

Had Priscilla known the depths of bitterness in Alec's soul, she would have lost the consolation of a doubt. But he kept his disappointment to himself. Priscilla's happiness was of greater moment than his own ambitions and he said nothing to destroy the sanctuary she had erected.

After completing his course in theology at Columbia Seminary, Alexander accepted a charge in South Carolina. He was able to schedule only short vacations in Mecklenburg. In a small Southern town the demands on a minister's time were persistent and incessant. The Palmetto State, even Alec was forced to admit, was a very pleasant place in which to live. Most of its leading families, like Alexander's own, were tempered with Hugenot blood. They knew how to make a gracious ceremony of living, the good works of the church included.

It was evident to Alec that Mr. Ney's stream of posterity for Priscilla's Price was rapidly running dry. The McIntosh breed would not stay put. From Scotland to Pennsylvania, from Pennsylvania to Mecklenburg and from Mecklenburg to South Carolina—all in less than a hundred years. Priscilla's Price was but a broken dam.

After twenty-odd years of careful nurture the place was now at its flower. Economically it had passed its prime, but aesthetically it neared perfection. The loveliness of the mansion-house was a balm to its builders resentful soul. The bricks had mellowed to a russet glow. Over them the small-leaf ivy, which Aunt Sally had brought from Rural Hill, had crept beneath the portico and festooned the iron balcony. From the queenly magnolias came the incense appropriate to Alec's temple to Priscilla. Although the Wilson box-wood had grown little, it had leafed out luxuriantly and hedged the parterres like borders for nosegays. The avenues formed walls of green in all directions. And the great black oaks, relics of Indian forests, shaded the house from summer's heat and considerately shed their leaves to let in the winter's sun.

The world could offer no prospect more beautiful to Alec than that from his own Indian hill. Green slopes, some in woods and some in cotton and grain, were trimmed with ribbons of red plantation roads. Down below, the mountain-born Catawba idled or frisked as the rains dictated, seeking an easy bed as had been its wont for countless centuries past.

The Piedmont had not only flowered. For the planters' way of life it had ripened. Already ambitous younger sons were moving to Alabama and Mississippi, where virgin lands were prodigal of their favors. It became increasingly difficult to make a large plantation in Carolina pay. Until recently the soil had asked little in return for its bounty, but each season now required deeper plowing and more fields left for fallow. Eroded clay and ruined wastes were costly. The cotton from such farms could not compete on even terms with the yield of the alluvial soil of the Gulf states.

Slave labor at best was improvident and inefficient. The patriarchal system of most Catawba planters was like man versus machine in competition with the coffled gangs of the Mississippi valley. The very old and the very young in the cabins represented a total loss in productivity, yet it had not occurred to Alec that a self-respecting planter could do anything about it. It was to the old and the young of his people that he felt the closest ties.

He had experimented briefly with other produce than the Southern staple but always with the same results. The Negroes planted, hoed and harvested every crop as though it were cotton, regardless of any resistant individualism. Changes complicated the overseer's routine and he was not interested in variety. Alec's efforts to get his people to grow their own food and weave their clothes had met with complacent non-cooperation. The darkies knew they would be clothed and fed anyway. For much of his corn meal, hog meat, cow peas and sorghum, Alec was accustomed to pay cash to the poor-whites. The mills in New England were turning out cheap cloth and he had no alternative but to buy it.

For the past few years Alec had been perplexed by the small net profit his cotton showed. As long as he had other lucrative investments, it had not greatly mattered. But the iron foundries were petering out. He had held his interest after other owners had withdrawn. For three generations it had been a family business. Alec was familiar with its operation and proud of its products. The era of the War of 1812, when the foundries supplied ammunition to the army, had witnessed flush times never regained. The timber supply for charcoal was nearing exhaustion. In Pennsylvania, mineral coal was abundant. Also the Yankees had railroads to their markets. Piedmont manufacturers reached the limit of their sales within a hundred miles. Slave labor was unsuited to the forge and white help demanded hard money. Few Southerners were hard money capitalists. The iron business would have to go.

Alec's bank stock had been wiped out by Andrew Jackson's war on the National Bank and the Panic of 1837. At least, that was the intelligence received from the Philadelphia bankers. Alec was too far away and too little versed in the law to undertake an investigation. He knew that the financial depression of '37 had impoverished many a man with nothing but money to his estate. After that, land seemed ever more essential. It was something your son could put his feet upon. But Alec's son was not a lover of the land.

His dilemma, Alec told himself, was less an emotional than a material problem. Land was dirt and a house was walls. Sentiment, like religion, was largely what you believed. And Priscilla had forsaken her faith in the former.

Should he take her to Alabama and start over? Many older than they were pulling up their roots and transplanting them in more generous soil. A removal, he knew, would be no violence to Priscilla now. She managed the household with methodical efficiency. That was her duty to her husband. But Priscilla had lost the happy whimsicality which had inspired the house. Her domestic plans were laid as meticulously as the rose petals and spices of her pot-pourri. All was in proper order, all essential ingredients were present. The result was genteel, restrained, slightly nostalgic, and, like the pot-pourri, dried of life. Priscilla's heart was no longer in the mansion on the hill. It beat now in the consecrated brick of Hopewell Church.

In spite of his wife's metamorphosis, Alec could not separate her from her home. It was the milieu for which she was made. When he thought of Priscilla he thought of Priscilla's Price, the frame designed for nature's work of art. He had built it for her because it was inevitable that someone should.

Although Priscilla had reached her forties, she had retained the grace that made her household gracious. And regardless of her detachment, Priscilla and Priscilla's Price could not be separated. Alec saw her as he rode home from the fields, standing beneath the massive portico softening its austerity like a Cherokee rose. Without her it was a monument, with her a civilization. Within a collection of treasures was transformed into a manner of life. He saw her in the rosewood chair by the fireside, her shoulders as elegantly erect as the garlanded chair back. He saw her across the leaves of the long banquet table, her reflection a portrait painted by candles in the polished walnut. He saw her on the sweep of the stairway, a hand and a handkerchief on the mahogany rail, the spirit of the house, in flesh and blood.

No. Alabama and Mississippi were for those whose roots were sick, for those whose hopes had withered. Priscilla was Priscilla's Price and Priscilla's Price was Priscilla. She must live in her temple as long as she lived on earth. If she failed to sense the unity, Alec did not. He would hold the house if it killed him. Mentally he took stock of the assets of the Valley.

Gold had been discovered in Mecklenburg about the year of his birth. The fever of speculation continued to afflict many of the inhabitants. In 1836 a Mint had been established in Charlotte. Northern and foreign capital was invested. Employment was provided for artisans, overseers and government agents. But no such homes as those from the cotton fields resulted.

Prophets of wealth from silk culture began to raise their voices. President Morrison of Davidson College was directed by the trustees to write a report on the importance of the new bonanza. Mulberry groves sprang up on many plantations. But the fad soon waned. A wedding gown or two and a few pair of elegant stockings were all that remained to mark its passing.

Such ephemeral dreams were not for Alec. From the land his fathers had reaped their livelihood and to the land Alec returned. Many of his fields were now past slave labor to redeem. He sold them off to the poor-whites. With each acre went a share of his vitality. He redoubled his efforts to make the remainder pay. The overseer was bought off with fifty acres across the River, and Alec assumed the duties of supervision himself. When he had a chance to sell a family of Negroes to a trust-worthy friend moving south, he sold them. Each sale took another reserve of strength. Only "nigger breeders" made a practice of selling slaves. Respectable planters, except in straightened circumstances, never sold their people. Alec swallowed the mortification and kept working.

The reduced plantation was put on a paying basis by careful husbanding and minute regulation. Crop rotation was found to be effective. Every idle field was sown in clover. The year following, the clover was turned under and the land used for cotton. Next wheat, then corn and back to clover. Peruvian guano was considered too expensive for cotton. But Alec discovered that when supplemented

by manure it would yield a narrow profit. Depleted red
clay was forced back into productivity.

Alec arose at daybreak and remained in the saddle
through sweltering heat or chilling rain. For the first time
in his life he carried a raw hide whip, but even the short
patience of fatigue never brought him to use it. When
Priscilla observed that his face looked drawn, he insisted
it was only the passing of time. When he tossed in his bed
and was unable to rest, he told her not to worry.

"At fifty," he said, "you don't need much sleep."

Yes, Alec would hold Priscilla's Price if it killed him.
And it did. Scipio was drilled in every detail of plantation
management. In place of an indulgent owner, he had now
a master who drove him as he drove himself. "You'll be the
driver when I'm gone" was drummed incessantly into the
Negro's brain.

Alec survived the strain for a few years, but his nerves
took out their spite on his heart. A paralyzing stroke gave
him warning but he ignored the threat as soon as his limbs
would obey his will. For the second assault there was no
resistance. Priscilla shared his pain for seven racking days.
Her own suffering at his bed side was doubled by her
realization of his motive. He never told her, but she knew.

"Scipio is a good foreman," he repeated. "By following
what he knows he can make the fields keep the house as
long as you live."

His last words were a knife in her heart.

"It's all right, darling. I won."

But Priscilla knew that she had lost. Would there be
no end to the price she must pay for her pride?

CHAPTER 23

ALEXANDER MCINTOSH, SENIOR, of Priscilla's Price was laid to rest in the family burying-ground on the plantation. The spot had been selected by the first Jeremiah. Here he and his hardworking spouse lay side by side beneath crude upright soapstones. For the second generation, Alec's parents, the granite slabs on miniature columns were embellished with the McIntosh coat of arms, or as Alec had said, with those of some forgotten dignitary of that ilk in Scotland. To mark the grave of little Sarah, Alec had secured an Agnus Dei. The symbolism of the marble lamb was a solace to Priscilla.

Except for the widow, the McIntosh name survived on the River only in chiseled stone.

The Reverend Alexander McIntosh of South Carolina conducted his father's funeral. As did his mother, Alexander strove for belief that Alec's faith had approximated the Presbyterian persuasion. So good a man should have no other. There was, however, no funeral sermon at Hopewell Church. For the sake of Priscilla, whose cousin he had married, the Reverend Hugh Cunningham would have preached it. But the odd request in Alec's will that only a specified quotation from the Episcopal *Book of Common Prayer* be inscribed on his tomb had set tongues wagging and placed the Hopewell minister in a delicate position.

The services were held at the burying-ground. In attendance were many from other counties to whom Priscilla had sent no black-ribboned invitations. Men whose names were scarcely known to Alexander, Junior, wore arm-bands of crape. Eulogies were pronounced in the unlettered lingo of the poor-whites and in the polished accent of Princeton. Throughout the reading of the scriptures there was an accompaniment of low moans from the Negroes.

On his return to South Carolina, Alexander sent from Charleston a marble monolith bearing only the name, birth and death dates of the deceased, and the epitaph chosen by himself:

"Ashes to ashes, Dust to dust."

Alec's body returned to the land to which he had given his life.

Priscilla resumed the routine of her existence at Priscilla's Price with a heavy heart. For her the conviction was now fixed that the house had cost her all the pain in her life. There had been the malediction of the Scotch elder at her infare when her heart was overflowing with anticipations of grandeur. There had been the sermon of the Reverend Samuel Caldwell on the eve of her housewarming. But the warnings had fallen on ears both stubborn and deaf. As a haughty daughter of Zion she had been smitten with a scab. Little Sarah was taken from her. And now Alec had bartered his life that her own should continue in a whited sepulcher.

On her return to the house from the burying-ground, she had doubled the mourning veil before her eyes to shut out the sight. But it was no use. Expiation demanded that she remain at Priscilla's Price. She had made her bed, bitter beauty though it was, and in it she must lie.

Alec urged his mother to sell the plantation and come to South Carolina. With all her heart she longed for the release, yet her conscience repelled the temptation. There were weak mortals in the Bible who had attempted to flee the path of duty. All had come to grief. And by act of Providence, or Nemesis, there was no market for Priscilla's Price. It was too elaborate for the acreage left to maintain it. No man without Alec's motive would sacrifice himself for such a vanity.

Priscilla yielded to her son's importunity to the extent of securing permanent house guests in Cousin Patience and Aunt Isabella.

Cousin Patience's husband had been murdered in a brawl, dignified as a duel since his antagonist also owned land. With her came her eighteen year old son, adapted by nature for his function of protector-apparent, and nothing else.

Aunt Isabella was actually a cousin of Mrs. Brevard. By reason of her step-father's remarriage to a woman younger than himself, she was legally without a home. In private she continued the no longer fashionable practice of snuffing, but aside from this dereliction was a model of all Hopewell virtues.

Neither of the women made demands on Priscilla's privacy. For a plantation mistress, bed and board could be provided without mental and economic demoralization.

Mrs. Brevard died in the erysipelas epidemic of 1845 which, with the aid of the physicians, took off a high percentage of Mecklenburg's white population. Her last years were devoted to supervising the upbringing of the fourteen offspring of a widowed niece, the constant child-bearing of whom had left her with what was euphemistically referred to in the family as a softening of the brain. Priscilla offered to adopt four of the orphans, but all efforts to separate the brood met with defeat. They were being reared by the Negroes they owned, and growing up to be models of deportment and piety.

Priscilla's sisters had married beyond the bounds of Hopewell and Unity. Her brothers, both unwed, kept bachelor quarters at Catawba Forge until its pre-Revolutionary timbers went up in flames. Without compunction, they moved into the yard office and lived with their books and dogs, oblivious to society.

For companionship, Priscilla came to depend on her numerous cousinry. If those in easy circumstances were most open in hospitality, she was not conscious of making distinctions. Their pretentious homes served as a balm to her troubled soul. In the decades which had elapsed since Priscilla's Price had aroused the resentment of the Presbyterian Piedmont, increasing prosperity had produced an amnesty. The McIntosh fortunes had flowered unseasonably. By now not a few cape jasmines had blossomed in the garb of gardenias.

Although Alec's mansion remained the Greek temple of the Catawba Valley, other planters had relaxed their fists with a generosity of gesture unconceived by the pioneers. From the cornucopia of cotton, blessings had poured over the Valley. Overnight, farmers became planters and found slavery ordained of God.

The hard times which confronted Alec had reduced many fortunes to more modest proportions. But the big houses remained. Upkeep, with a yard full of pickaninnies and silver-pated dependents, was chiefly a matter of energetic oversight. And cotton went up when Europe went to war.

Priscilla had few responsibilities at home. During Alec's last years Scipio had been well indoctrinated as foreman of the twenty-five remaining field hands. Scipio's future if the place were sold was another claim on Priscilla's conscience. She had rejected as affronts to her obligations fabulous sums offered for his purchase. In moulding a foreman, Alec had cast for his hopes a better anchor than he knew.

The deadening flow of life at Priscilla's Price was interrupted for Priscilla only by visits to her kin. There was warrant for this in the Scriptures. The early Christians visited much with their brethren in the faith. If the escape thus provided alone prevented an overwhelming morbidity in her thoughts she would not admit its significance. To do so would countenance a fleeing from duty. But once the carriage was headed outward, her eyes never turned back toward the proud pile behind.

Of the genteel seats, Ingleside in Lincoln County most closely approached Priscilla's Price. With Ionic columns and pediment designed by the architect Latrobe, it had been the gossip of the community and the eventual ruin of the Forneys who built it. Priscilla had known intimately the three families which had successively struggled against its baleful possession.

Built shortly after Alec's exotic in Mecklenburg, Ingleside had exacted of Major Daniel Forney obligations which he was unwilling to assume. Since the Major had married Harriet Brevard, Priscilla and Alec were amongst those expected for the week-long celebrations of political and domestic triumphs. Daniel Forney had represented his district in Congress and received Alec's friendship and approval until his decision to desert the state of his birth for Alabama. Regardless of whatever justification the Major had for his removal, Alec never forgave him. From then on "as fickle as a Forney" became his characteristic condemnation for lack of persistence.

A visionary son of Judge William Gaston became the next master of Ingleside which he rechristened Ravenna.

Like his father, Alexander Gaston read widely, wrote poetry and was a charming conversationalist. Priscilla found that his Huguenot consanguinity outweighed the obstacle to friendship of his Catholic education, a social barrier to many in the Piedmont. The gentle ways of the Carolina coast came to the up-country with the Gastons. And the frescoed parlour of Ravenna bid fair to become the Catawba Valley's first literary salon. But the promise was never fulfilled. In less than two years Eliza Gaston lay beneath Unity churchyard's most elaborate gravestone inscribed with her husband's tribute to her virtues:

Pulchritudine felix, mente clarior, vita colendissima.

During the period of Priscilla's widowhood, Ingleside was owned by a Scotchman named James Anderson. Although he had married a sister of Alfred and Robert Burton of Lincoln, Mr. Anderson showed no disposition to live up to the pretensions of his house. The Burtons, having produced a governor of the state, were now firmly entrenched as a Catawba Valley first family and James and Elizabeth Anderson might easily have assumed a leadership in plantation society. Their failure to do so, singularly enough, was resented by many in Unity as a defaulting of obligations.

Priscilla had nothing but approbation for the Ingleside of the Andersons. Its Ionic elegance, to her thinking, was far better graced by Polyhymnia than by the Forney's Terpsichore or the Gaston's Euterpe. Between herself and Elizabeth Burton, sorrow cemented the bond of affection. The one surviving child of the house was a frail and high-strung youth. That he be spared for the Presbyterian ministry was the constant prayer of his parents. Priscilla's petitions were joined to those of her hosts.

The earthy aspirations of the Forneys and of Priscilla's

own youth seemed now as sand to the rock of the Andersons' faith. In the familiar lines of the Portuguese hymn was reflected Priscilla's joy in her visits to Ingleside:

> How firm a foundation, ye saints of the Lord
> Is laid for your youth in His excellent word.

Close by the River, a few miles from Ingleside, was the Georgian mansion of the Grahams. The long lane that led to Elm Wood Farm was frequently travelled by Priscilla's carriage. There was a time-defying quality about the solid brick walls of the homestead, as though the Grahams intended to sit in this seat for eternity. Like Ingleside, the mansion was built on a fortune in iron and the River portico was chiefly constructed of that element. But John D. Graham, son of General Joseph, laid out his inheritance in fields and slaves and became one of the great planters of the Piedmont. His brothers had chosen preferment in the professions, but John had chosen the land. The Catawba washed the steps of his porch and as far as the eye could see watered the bottoms of his plantation.

Life amongst the young was gay at Elm Wood. In its marbleized ballroom many a timid and fantastic toe tripped for the first time the waltz and the polka. Priscilla's conscience could not condone these face-to-face innovations. She was thankful that Alexander had been safely consecrated to the ministry before such flesh and the devil temptations had been invented. The reels and minuets, however worldly, had been exhibitions in grace and form.

"These new jiggumbobs," observed a pious black crone, "ain't nothing but white folks hugging to music like niggers."

But the embers of Calvinism still tempered the recreations of the older Grahams and the Unity ministers were honored guests at Elm Wood. Priscilla continued her visits and prayed for clemency for its frequent frivolity.

The third of the big houses in the Lincoln County cousinry was Mount Tirzah of the Brevards. An atavistic evidence of French forebears crept curiously out in the three doors across both front and rear of the great clap-boarded mansion. Within, the traditions of the Huguenots had left their mark of noblesse oblige. The exceptionally beautiful daughters of the house had made exceptionally brilliant matches. During summer vacations, Mount Tirzah became the gathering place of in-law statesmen, scholars and men of fashion.

"Law, Miss 'Scilla," Thalia confided to her mistress, "des Low-country niggers what Marse Hayne brings up here am a case."

"How's that, Thalia?" Priscilla asked.

"I hearn one of dem braggin' about Miss Harriet's grand-daddy gettin' hung on de gallus in Cha'ston. I done told her we ain't had none o' our folks strung up and if we is we ain't braggin' 'bout it."

Priscilla smiled. "Colonel Isaac Hayne was hanged by the British during the Revolution. His patriotism made his execution honorable."

The perplexity of the Negroes concerning the Hayne martyrdom was paralleled in her own mind with respect to the South Carolinians' condonation of duelling. There had been few "affairs of honor" in the Piedmont and the ministers took advantage of its relative rarity to preach against the practice on Biblical grounds. Some of the younger Brevards, however, had become converts to the South Carolinians' code punctilio. Cousin Theodorous Brevard, who had moved to Alabama, was once involved in such an affair. The older members of the family agreed with Priscilla, but the young hotspurs were quick to resent the suggestion that any alternative with honor was open to Theodorous.

"After all, Cousin Priscilla," one of them told her with finality, "the duel was divinely instituted when David fought Goliath."

Educated, opulent and debonaire, the Brevards nevertheless retained their standing as Presbyterian pillars. Old Captain Alex of the Revolution left the imprint of Center on the Unity congregation. Revivals and infidelity he viewed with equal distaste. Under his roof, French Deism might be discussed only if it gave no offence to other guests present. The liberality of his hospitality continued after his death. Priscilla was entertained at Mount Tirzah with a courtesy unsurpassed in the Piedmont.

C H A P T E R 24

CLOUD OVER CATAWBA

ALTHOUGH BORN and bred in Lincoln County, the Widow McIntosh had more relatives in Hopewell Congregation than in Unity. Her mother's people had taken literally the Biblical injunction to fructification and multiplication. For several weeks each year Priscilla fled the pall over Priscilla's Price and occupied a guest chamber in the Rural Hill homestead of her grandfather. The old patriarch, common progenitor of most of Priscilla's prosperous cousinry, had run his course at ninety-seven and earned his rest in the burying-ground in view of his mansion.

The house had been brought into the mode by the alteration of its hip roof to one with gable ends. But the place never lost the charm it had held for Priscilla's girlhood. The iron filigree grill between the cement covered columns bespoke its affinity with Ingleside, Elm Wood and Mount Tirzah as a monument to the industry founded by its builder.

Here, too, Priscilla sensed a relaxing of the Presbyterian mores amongst the young. For the elders, Biblical themes were still a weeknight as well as a Sabbath topic for dissertation, a favorite being the eventual return of the Jews to Palestine. The interest was not inappropriate. Neither affluence nor intermarriage with Wilsons, Brevards and Springs had abated the acquisitive enterprise of the Rural Hill cousins. When the boys weren't attending Davidson College they were put to the plow or broad-axe along with the half a hundred slaves of the plantation. Uncle Jacky followed the laborers to the fields. While they hoed cotton he improved their minds with questions from the Shorter Catechism. No use letting faculties lie idle.

"The best way to take care of your conscience," he told Priscilla, "is to tire it out. You never heard of a darkey worried about his soul. By the time they get to meeting all they can do is praise God for the rest."

The strenuosity of the household left Priscilla little time for introspective brooding. Uncle Jacky could stand on his porch and call his slaves two miles away. Everybody attended early morning prayers. They worked hard, played hard and worshipped hard. To die at Rural Hill at less than eighty indicated a puny specimen of the breed.

Priscilla included in her migrations the Holly-wood and Oak Lawn plantations of the sons of Rural Hill. Age had relieved their once envied mansions of pretense. The reflection brought a fleeting solace, but Priscilla's Price, she knew, was built to the scale of ancient arrogance.

Oak Lawn was approached by an avenue shaded for over a mile with oaks and cedars. Enclosing the domestic yard was the handsomest wall of open-faced brick in Mecklenburg. Gossip maintained that Uncle Ben had intended the brick for his homestead but that a quarrel with his Torrance neighbors whose house was brick had changed his mind. The vaunted medium was good enough for his fence and no more. His mansion-house was frame, clapboarded and dazzling white, and second to none in the Valley. All that was long ago. Later frame houses had eclipsed the ambitious effort. Uncle Ben was dead and his sons had gone courting at the Torrances' Cedar Grove.

Priscilla sighed as she thought of the passion spent on such futility. She said a prayer for the soul of her misguided uncle. In the great beyond of how little consequence were the scenic wallings and pedimented overmantels of his earthly habitat? Had he heeded in his last days the warning placed in epitaph upon his tomb?

Attentive reader let my mouldering clay
Wake your reflection while tis called today.
Tis time I'm gone thou'rt going and soon thine head
Will softly recline among the silent dead.
Art thou prepared; where will thy spirit be
When time is lost in vast Eternity?

Priscilla did not know. She could only hope and rejoice
that in the son who inherited the mansion, Oak Lawn had
found a master who was a consecrated elder in Hopewell Church.

At Holly-wood, Aunt Peggy, born an Osborne of Belmont, was proverbial for the milk of human kindness, a
fortunate asset since Uncle Robin's virtues were not so
mollified. In worldly attainments he had outstripped his
kith and kin and was the only planter in Mecklenburg to
work a hundred slaves. His steep white mansion-house with
its narrow windows was beginning to look old-fashioned.
But to Priscilla's altered standards it had now a better
claim to veneration. Since Uncle Robin and Aunt Peggy
had no children, the orphaned overflow of brothers and
sisters found a home beneath their roof. Uncle Robin saw
to it that the boys earned their keep, but the affectionate
nature of his better half was lavished without stint on her
own and in-law nieces and nephews.

During one of Priscilla's visits to Holly-wood several of
the boys who had volunteered for the Mexican war came
to bid their aunt goodbye.

"Will there have to be fighting?" she asked.

Her nephews thought there would.

"Well, if there is," she replied, "I hope nobody will get
hurt."

Aunt Peggy was born without toes, but she trod this
world on the feet of angels.

Glenwood, the plantation of Cousin Alex Caldwell, had, perhaps, the least pretentious mansion-house of any of the homes Priscilla frequented.

"While other men cultivate their lands," it was said of the owner, "Alex Caldwell cultivates his mind."

There was a restful, homey quality about the rectangular house, with its long piazza, that endeared it to Priscilla more than many a mansion of wealthier kin. Most Catawba plantations had libraries but that at Glenwood was a part of the life of the house.

"Priscilla," said her cousin as she stepped out of the carriage, "come in the parlour while Scipio unpacks and let me read you a poem."

Cousin Alex was in dignified transports over a small volume just received from New York entitled *Catawba River and Other Poems.*

"I do not know who Mr. John Steinford Kidney may be," said Priscilla's host, "but he has written a beautiful tribute to our River. Listen to the opening verse:

With oaken pillars yonder height is strong,
    To which the bristling pines are clambering.
Beneath—Catawba frets, and speeds along:—
    The softened roar is asking me to sing:
And, river! thou shalt move this day
    Through this, I think, thy virgin lay.

"It is very lovely," Priscilla said. She followed its gentle flow through twenty-nine verses.

"When I was young," Cousin Alex concluded, "I delighted in the scenery of the old country as pictured in the poems of Byron, Scott and Burns. Now that I am getting old myself I enjoy most the poetry of the new

world in which we live, especially a piece about our own
red hills and river."

"Philo Henderson," Priscilla suggested, "has some beautiful verse on the Catawba in *The Hornets' Nest.*"

"Yes," Cousin Alex agreed. "I have preserved his 'Flower
of Catawba' from the paper. I knew the Hendersons when
they lived at Davidson College. Philo is a sensitive writer
but of frail constitution for journalism. I doubt that he will
live to achieve his full stature as a poet. But we should
cherish what he has given us.

"By the by, Priscilla, here is a new book on the Puritans
you will read with profit. It's remarkable how much more
the faith of our fathers resembled that of Cromwell than
the Cavaliers."

As an authority on ecclesiastical history, Alexander Caldwell had few peers outside the ministry. His brilliant mind
accepted the tenets of Christianity with the credulity of
a child.

"Alex Caldwell," his brother once observed, but not in
Priscilla's hearing, "is a very remarkable man. He and I
have the same heredity, the same education, the same
environment. He reads his Bible daily, as I once did myself, and believes it all. Whereas I, I don't believe a damn
word of it."

If the contrast between the calm assurance of Glenwood
and her restless life at home made Priscilla weep for release
from her penance, it was owing to no lack of charity on
the part of her host.

The "Princeton Alexanders" still lived at Rosedale. Dr.
Joe had preceded Alec McIntosh to the grave and his son,
Dr. Winslow, had followed soon after. Dr. Winslow's wi-
dow, a daughter of General Joseph Graham of Vesuvius

Furnace, welcomed Priscilla like a sister. In place of the old brick house there was now a large frame dwelling with a double gallery.

"Rosedale reminds me of South Carolina," Priscilla told her cousin. "So many of the homes where Alexander preaches have second story porches, and so few do in Mecklenburg."

"The girls enjoy sitting on the gallery at bed time," said Violet Alexander, "and singing. Salem gives them excellent training."

"And the Lord," added Priscilla, "gave them lovely voices. I hope I may hear them tonight."

The night turned out to be chilly and the song-feste was held in the parlour. The Alexanders' pianoforte was kept faultlessly in tune.

"Shall we play first, Cousin Priscilla," the girls asked, "and then sing?"

"Yes, do, dears," Priscilla replied. "Play anything you like."

"We learned the Hayden and Handel overtures at Salem," the girls announced, and they took turns rendering the spirited music.

Next came the marches. "These are fun," the girls laughed. "Isn't it *distingué* to have a special march to your own grandfather? The Salem Band played it at the May 20th celebration in '35." The performers executed a duet arrangement of "General Graham's March."

"I remember it well," Priscilla reminisced. "Also Uncle Joseph's oration on the same occasion. He told about the original signing he had witnessed as a lad. The people gave him a tremendous ovation. There was also a march to General Polk."

"We learned that one, too," the girls said. "And also 'The Mecklenburg Grand March'." They played both with gusto and many improvised flourishes.

Priscilla's thoughts ran back to the gala celebration, to Alexander's delight in the colorful uniforms, and to her debonair husband trying so hard to give her a good time. With an effort she held back the tears.

Violet Alexander sensed her cousin's sadness. She knew that not all music evokes a corresponding tempo of emotion. In her life, also, there were gay songs which brought more pain than pleasure.

"Why not try a few numbers from the Minstrel Shows?" she suggested to her daughters.

The girls changed easily from the martial marches to "Ethiopian serenades." In the North they had found the black-faced comedians more diverting than their Southern originals.

"We don't know whose songs we like best, Cousin Priscilla," they said, "Dan Emmett's or Stephen Foster's. We'll let you decide."

They sang first Emmett's "Old Dan Tucker" and "The Blue-Tailed Fly." Then followed the nostalgic Foster melodies "Old Uncle Ned" and "Oh Susannah." Priscilla had polite applause for all four.

"Good musicians," said Violet Alexander, "like those at Salem, don't approve this minstrel music. But I have a feeling that some day Mr. Emmett and Mr. Foster are going to compose songs that the South will never let die."

"Alec would have agreed with you," Priscilla remarked. "He used to let the Negroes sing spirituals after prayers. And more than once I heard him tell company from up North, 'That's the heart of the South you hear.' I used to think it far-fetched, but now I think he was right."

The girls were too much a part of the South to appreciate its individuality. This was old-folks' talk. Music might be the voice of an emotion but hardly of a place.

"How do you like the new hymn tunes of Lowell Mason?" the girls asked. "Our teacher at Salem says he is liberating the American churches from the fugue."

"I was reared on the old ones, my dears," Priscilla replied, "but I would love to hear you sing the new. Mr. Mason had a devoted following in Savannah and a number of our younger ministers think very highly of his music."

The girls' soft altos blended in the soothing rhythms of "Jesus Lover Of My Soul," "Safely Through Another Week" and "I Sing The Almighty Power Of God."

Priscilla sighed wistfully. "No doubt our grandchildren will hold to these tunes as our grandmothers did the original ones. So it goes. You were good to sing them for me. And now, which of the modern songs do you like best?"

The girls laughed a little shyly. "They aren't hymns, Cousin Priscilla. You'd think we were too sentimental."

"At your age you have a right to be a little. I think the Lord made girls sentimental to keep them sweet. Could I hear them? And then an old lady must snuff her candle for the night."

The haunting melodies of the favorites of the day filled the parlour. How soon, thought Priscilla, must "Long, Long Ago" recall to those who now sang it such a night as this at Rosedale. Nowhere was "Ben Bolt" sung with more poignancy or "Home, Sweet Home" with more propriety.

CHAPTER 25

CLOUD OVER CATAWBA

THE CATAWBA VALLEY had been kind to Priscilla. Beloved by the privileged circle in which she moved and respected by the periphery of those less fortunate, she had achieved a place which no mere wealth or circumstance could have commanded. And yet, at fifty she was a lonely woman.

Relatives and friends with guests to flatter or impress brought them to visit the stately mansion and gardens which Scipio's supervision maintained in ordered elegance. Few departed without a trace of envy, none with any conception of the burden a heart's desire could lay upon a heart which no longer desired it.

The very perfection of the place served to remind Priscilla of the price she had paid to obtain it. Alec had given his life, almost his soul, for this conceit of her girlhood. If the unbelieving husband were sanctified by the wife it was Priscilla's obligation to save him from perdition. She must so live that God would forgive in Alec those imperfections for which she blamed herself. With a wife in his youth less vain of this world might he not have been turned toward the other?

Her reflections turned logically to herself. Without Alec where would her path have led? If not Priscilla McIntosh, who would she have been? Her early marriage had precluded the accumulation of conquests. An unfrequented corner of her consciousness was lighted by the glow of an antiquated blue stone. She was suddenly aware that no longer need she fear to let in her thoughts. For a widow there was retrospection not lawful for a wife. Had she hurt Peter McClelland with her thoughtless coquetry? How had he acquired the earring and why had he preserved it? For what reason, after fifteen years, had he thrown it aside? The lodge had not been built when she lost the bauble and Urania had found it conspicuously on the floor.

Small incidents of past years linked themselves in explanation: his visits to Catawba Forge before her marriage, her father's interest in sending him to Tennessee, his failure to call when her betrothal was announced but rumors that he was at home, the hostility of his sister and family, his long state of celibacy and his painful reserve on the night he had spent in her home.

Wanton eyes and a stretched forth neck had indeed been hers to deceive one anointed of the Lord. And smitten by God she had been. He was now free. On the night the stars fell he had cast the stone aside. The miracle had achieved his release. But of her own sin? Was there yet forgiveness in heaven for her heedless mincing? If Peter McClelland had forgiven her, perhaps God also would blot out her iniquity. She must know the truth from the minister himself.

Frequent notices of the activities of Reverend Mr. McClelland appeared in the church papers. Throughout the West there was no preacher more widely heralded for his frontier awakenings. Priscilla had seen mention of the Arkansas post where his services were current. She would write him for absolution.

Her letter was composed with great care. To claim an importance in his past was itself a vanity. If her forebodings were correct, and by now she had no doubt, he would understand without a direct allusion. She wrote merely as a friend of long standing to ask his prayers for the sins of her youth. With these, she reminded him, he was better acquainted than anyone now left alive. She mentioned Alexander's work in South Carolina and her joy in her son's high calling.

For several weeks Priscilla waited expectantly for a reply. But none came. Was it possible he could not forgive her? Not once since the memorable night in '33 had she seen or heard from him. He had written only a courteous reply to Alec. If he had revisited Lincoln County she did not know it. Both parents were dead and all surviving brothers and sisters, except Melissa, had migrated west. He had few ties in Carolina.

By the end of the month Priscilla was convinced that another weight had been added to her already overburdened conscience. If the Reverend Peter McClelland held her guilty, the Lord would not easily forget her transgressions. In distress of spirit she spent much time in her chamber in meditation and prayer.

From her window she sought a solace in the meandering Catawba below. Despite the fall rains, the widening flood flowed smoothly through the bottoms. A mile upriver a raft appeared. Priscilla watched it intently. It was poled by a single passenger. Why should her breath become short and her heartbeats quick? Many a voyager took advantage of the free propulsion of the current. She left the window and lay down on the bed to quiet the sudden throbs.

Half an hour elapsed before Priscilla heard the voice of Thalia at the door.

"Miss 'Scilla, you'se got a caller in de parlour."

Priscilla glanced into the mirror to tidy herself. A slender matron with a lavender stole about her shoulders returned her scrutiny. For her age she was incongruously beautiful. No streaks of grey deadened the sheen of her hair and no hint of time dimmed the brown luster of her eyes. The lines in her face were lines of loveliness. An unaccountable tear brightened her lashes.

"I saw your raft upriver," she greeted her guest as though they had parted yesterday.

The middle-aged minister stood with the confused silence of the boy Peter.

Priscilla smiled as she had the day he called for the lumber. For all his fame, he was still the uncertain young man who paid unconscious compliments. In the span of time which separated them from youth, she had addressed his memory as the Reverend Mr. McClelland. The formality fell away with the years.

"Peter," she said, "I hope you have forgiven me."

He took her outstretched hand and pressed it to his lips. With a half light, half bitter retort, he obliterated the past, "There's no fool like an old fool."

They sat in the parlour and talked until night. Cousin Patience and Aunt Isabella passed through the hall unnoticed. Priscilla found an ease of confidence she rarely experienced, and Peter's reticence was melted by her sympathy. More than once when his revelations were deeply personal he asked her permission for a brief word of prayer. "It is promised," he said, "that God will succor those whose sole reliance is in Him." Both had suffered long for conscience' sake. And each to the other was innocent of wrong.

"You are generous and kind, Peter," Priscilla said, "but I cannot forgive myself for the pain I have inflicted on others."

"Your youth is more than atoned for," he consoled her.

"You must forget those things which are behind. It would be my greatest happiness, next to my service to my God, to devote the rest of my life to yours."

The flush of fifteen suffused the face of the woman of fifty. She shook her head.

"We are old people, Peter," her voice was pathetically young, "too old to start life anew. You have your work to which I can contribute little, and I have duties here which I could not in conscience desert."

"No, Priscilla," he differed gently, "we are only old in the flesh from which God has released us. We are young in the spirit of Christ. Through trials and tribulations God has made us meet for His work together. I will not press you. Think and pray and I will come tomorrow for your answer—and for His."

In Priscilla's desk was an admonitory letter from her son. It had meant little to her when received but after Peter left she sought it hopefully for guidance.

"You are far too young, Mother," Alexander had written, "to live a lonely life. Father would not expect of you the sacrifice you are making. He lived for your happiness as he understood it, and he would want it now. You could do his memory no greater honor than to choose a suitable companion for your latter years. I wish with all my heart that you would remarry."

Six months ago the letter had brought a smile to Priscilla. It now brought tears. Was Alexander only her selfless son, or had he as a man of God the wisdom to advise her?

It was ten o'clock when she completed her letter and addressed it to the South Carolina manse. The household was still in sleep as she closed the secretary to retire. A knock on the door surprised her. Could it be Peter?

Not yet had her silent prayers been answered. God still withheld the light of His countenance from her and the vigil of the night lay ahead. Unless He spoke with unmistakable assurance, her life and Priscilla's Price were one.

She opened the door and was accosted by Peter's sister Melissa.

"Good even', Mrs. McIntosh. I know it's late but I got to see you now."

"Of course, my dear. Come in." Priscilla led her into the parlour.

"I ain't got time to set down," Melissa declined Priscilla's gesture. "If you don' min' I'll have my say and get goin'. I didn't come on no social visit and don' never expect to here, but you ain't to blame for that, leastaways not as you can help."

"Feel free to speak as you wish. If you will forgive me I will sit. Today has not been easy."

"That's what I thought and that's why I'm here. It ain't been easy for Peter neither. He axed you to marry him, didn't he?"

"I think you had best discuss that with your brother." Priscilla forgot her invitation to frankness and started to rise.

"Now don' get huffy with me, please, Mrs. McIntosh. We're plain speakin' people, us McClellands and Peter's one of us. You'd never think like us nor us like you. I'd talk to Peter but he ain't rational about you—never was since he got hair on his face."

Priscilla settled weakly in her chair.

"I don' know for what reason you might take him now, Mrs. McIntosh, but for his sake don' do it. People say you've los' your pleasure in this place, but it's part o' you like a preacher's stan's part o' Peter. His preachin's for his own kin', not for yourn. If you brought him here it 'ud kill him. If you went wi'd him people 'ud hear about this place acrost the Mississippi. The knowin' of it w'ud ruin him wi'd husbans whose wives was brung up to wait on 'em and wi'd women what don' know no better. To put it plain, Mrs. McIntosh, you took this on your own choosin', don' take from Peter what he took on his'n.

"Goodnight, Mrs. McIntosh."

Melissa had closed the front door before Priscilla regained her feet. She stood a few moments in indecision; then she walked over to the desk and removed her letter to Alexander from its pigeon-hole. His advice was no longer necessary. She tore through the envelope and dropped the pieces between the smoldering logs. Seating herself again at the secretary, she wrote rapidly to Peter McClelland.

> Kindest and most cherished friend,
>
> Through whatever instruments God makes known His will He leaves us in no doubt when He speaks. My place, I know now, is here. I will not pretend that there can be peace in my heart in a house whose very shadow is an accusation. But as you value my salvation do not turn me from it.
>
> I thank you, Peter, for all that you said. No mortal can do more for me than you have done. The recollection of it will help to keep me strong. May my gratitude suffice for you.
>
> God go with you,
Priscilla McIntosh.

Early in the morning she sent her reply by Scipio to the house of Peter's sister where he lodged. She wrote again to Alexander, but her letter was concerned with his anticipated visit to Mecklenburg in the Spring.

CHAPTER 26

CLOUD OVER CATAWBA

MAY 20, 1850, was eagerly awaited by Priscilla. Despite its anniversary significance, it would not, however, be a day of mark for the County. The people were behind in their crops and few would feel able to come in from the country. Only the Independent Order of Odd Fellows was sponsoring much of a celebration for the seventy-fifth milestone in Mecklenburg's independence.

There was to be a procession with the members of Declaration Lodge in full regalia, a reading of Mecklenburg's historic document and an address by one of the brotherhood at the Church. After that the members would repair to Major Jennings Kerr's Carolina Inn and doubtless feast on the establishment's famous chicken pies, cooked in yellow queensware dishes. There would be toasts to the Polks, the Alexanders and the Brevards.

But it was not for this that Priscilla's heart beat faster. On Sunday, the day after the celebration, the Reverend Alexander McIntosh, D.D., would preach in Charlotte. It seemed a consummation of all of Priscilla's hopes for twenty-five long, unhappy years. Her son would stand before his people in the pulpit of their God; he would recall their obligations to the Fountain of all blessings.

Priscilla and Alexander were entertained in the home of Dr. David T. Caldwell, a few miles from Charlotte on the Salisbury highway. Dr. David, being brothers' sons with Cousin Alex of Glenwood, was in Priscilla's family circle, though no blood relation of her own. His marriage to one of the Frew connection had brought him the finest frame house in the vicinity of the village.

"It's been over five years," the Doctor remarked to his guests, "since Alexander has paid his county seat the compliment of a visit."

"It's been six and a half, I'm ashamed to say," the minister admitted. "But Mother's been down to see me, you know."

"And Charlotte still is his county seat," Priscilla declared, "though I have my doubts he'll recognize it. I can't help thinking how different is the town today from the struggling cross roads of a similar occasion twenty-five years ago." Priscilla had attended several interim celebrations but May 20, 1825, with its tragic aftermath stood starkly in her memory.

"Well, our progress is chiefly quality and not quantity," Dr. Caldwell explained. "I noticed in the courthouse the other day that we claimed seven hundred inhabitants in '25 and we've just about passed the thousand mark this year. But appearances have considerably altered."

He looked at Priscilla and smiled.

"The dress Charlotte wears today is as far from the skimpy drapery you wore as a belle as are those umbrella crinolines."

Priscilla, of course, was shrouded in black. She wore the flowing weeds of widowhood and expected to do so until she died. No less was becoming in Presbyterian relicts with proper respect for their husbands' memory. She had, however, conceded to fashion to the extent of a boned bodice and half a dozen stiffened petticoats of paper muslin. If skirts continued to widen it would not be long before hoops would be essential to hold them up.

"Speaking of the courthouse,' said Alexander, "I'm anxious to see the new one. Mecklenburg, like all the South, appears to have gone Grecian."

"We'll see that, the rebuilt Mint, and anything else you've missed, in the morning," Dr. Caldwell assured him. "I told Icarus to bring the carriage immediately after breakfast so we can drive around before you go to the church."

"The town has some fine buildings," Priscila remarked, "but no home as lovely as this." It was true. The best dwellings of the Mecklenburgers were still outside the county seat.

"Ever since Mr. Frew built this house," Priscilla continued, "I've loved its dormers, its high center and low wings. It's like the homes in tidewater Virginia without their pretense and pride."

"I'd hardly put it in the class with Priscilla's Price," her host observed with a twinkle.

"And for that," Priscilla returned solemnly, "you should be eternally grateful to God."

"Before we turn in tonight," Alexander changed the subject, "let's walk up and take a look at old Sugaw Creek."

Dr. Caldwell agreed. "Our brick church isn't as fine as your Hopewell, but it's a great improvement over the log-meeting-house in which my father preached."

"Not only your father," Priscilla added, "but your grandfather, too."

"No," said Alexander, "the Reverend Alexander Craighead preached in an earlier log house. I remember hearing father say that when he went to school to Dr. Caldwell's father there were remnants of the old Craighead church still left."

By the time they reached Sugaw Creek it was almost dusk. Alexander took out his memorandum book to copy inscriptions from some of the early tombstones. To Mecklenburgers the hallowed spot was almost Holy Ground. Here the pioneer Craighead had first sown the seeds of gospel independence. At the two great sassafras trees which marked the grave of the Father of Mecklenburg Independence, Alexander said a prayer of thanksgiving.

"It's too bad," remarked Dr. Caldwell, "that my vindicated ancestor can't be present tomorrow."

"He will be there," replied Priscilla, "in the spirit."

On the morning following, the Caldwells and their guests took an early seat behind the Doctor's spanking brace of bays and drove into the village. The nip of May put the charges of Icarus in fine fettle. It was with difficulty that he held them down for his master's passing observations.

North Tryon Street, housing city-bred folk, was only beginning to offer its incense of Sunday breakfast.

"The jail," Alexander observed as they drove by, "is still the most imposing structure on Charlotte's main street. I'm afraid that doesn't speak too well for a law-abiding citizenry."

"On the contrary," replied his host, "the center of town has now shifted to the vicinity of the Presbyterian church. That ought to indicate a change of heart. For fifty years, you know, Charlotte had no church at all."

The carriage turned the corner at Trade Street, opposite Leroy Springs' large store, the handsomest in the village. The broad expanse of West Trade was cleared of shadows by the morning sun.

"It could almost be said," Dr. Caldwell pointed out, "that Charlotte is epitomized on the corner of Trade and Church Streets. We have the Courthouse, the Church and the Mint in close communion."

"Religion, law and thrift," the minister agreed. "A good Scotch-Irish heritage. May Charlotte ever be so distinguished."

He observed the three symbols with interest. The church was little changed from his earliest recollections. It occupied the center of a large square; and though not as old as Alexander himself, its unornamented brick appeared singularly old-fashioned beside the cement covered Mint and white columned courthouse.

"With this craze for stucco," Dr. Caldwell remarked, "it probably won't be long before we plaster over the church and add a cathedral spire."

"Aunt Sally wouldn't approve it," Priscilla recollected with charitable humor, "but a steeple for the church seems one of the few ambitions of my youth I still entertain. If it offends the older members, though, it shouldn't be pressed."

"I doubt you'd have the opposition," Alexander remarked, "that the introduction of hymns aroused in your grandfathers' day or that organs did a generation later."

"The Charlotte church has survived both heresies," Dr. Caldwell observed. "In this day of railroads, daguerreotypes and street lamps nothing seems impossible."

The driver pulled the carriage to a halt in front of the church.

"Tie the horses in the field below the Mint," his master told him. "I won't need you for several hours, but keep an eye on the carriage if you value your skin."

Icarus gave him a deferential "Yassur" and felt in his pocket for his good-luck "bones." There might even be a cock-fight down on the creek. Sunday was a good day.

"I left word with Scipio," Priscilla remembered, "to meet

us here after services. He wanted to hear Alexander preach but I don't believe he can get in in time."

"I meant to tell you yesterday," her host remarked, "that we could easily have put up Scipio and taken care of the horses. Icarus told me he had started for home before I could speak to him."

"It was his own decision," Priscilla replied. "Nothing will keep him away from the place over Saturday night. He's afraid of trouble in the quarters since the unfortunate episode of Mr. Cook."

All that Priscilla knew respecting Mr. Cook, the schoolmaster, was that he had been forced to flee the county for inciting the Negroes. Actually, the slave patrol had caught him abed with a dusky concubine. White men of respectability didn't go to Negro cabins for such purposes. When the culprit identified himself as the schoolteacher, his captors feigned disbelief. Mr. Cook wasn't white trash, they told him. He was a mulatto passing himself off as the teacher. For his imposture he was given thirty-nine lashes and a warning to make his face scarce. On the same night the schoolmaster disappeared.

Scipio's alarm was doubtless unfounded, but any disturbance that savored of abolitionism excited him to vigilance. The lot of free niggers was no condition to be preferred to foreman of Priscilla's Price.

"Poor, faithful Scipio," Priscilla sighed. "He feels all the responsibility for the place that Alec did. It shouldn't be his cross to bear, just because it's mine."

"I'm sure he doesn't so consider it, Mother," her son comforted her. "To Scipio, serving you may be his crown."

CHAPTER 27

THE GILT EAGLE above the Mint's portico glistened in the sun. Alexander suggested that they walk over for a closer view.

"I'm very much surprised," he said, "at the success of the Mint. Father always considered the gold mines a flash in the pan."

"Over $360,000 was coined there last year," Dr. Caldwell told him. "But your father was right. Few of the miners ever got rich."

"Not even the Chevalier de Frenoli?" Priscilla asked.

"He put up a big front," Dr. Caldwell replied, "marble mantels and oil lamp chandeliers in his house and a mulatto barber to dress his hair, but the money belonged to the British investors who sent him here to head the company. As a matter of fact, I don't know one substantial family in the county with a fortune in gold."

"I wrote you, Alexander," his mother remarked, "about the conversion of Captain Penman." The latter was the oddest of the exotic crew which the gold miners had attracted to Mecklenburg. The Captain arrived from England accompanied by his white body servant and two uncertain females whom he passed off as his sisters. After a period of riotous living and ruinous mining, he abandoned gold for the ministry to the gratification of the Methodists and his financial backers.

Dr. Caldwell directed Alexander's attention to the new courthouse which stood on the corner east of the church. The neo-classic temple had replaced the cupola-topped structure on the Square the same year the Mint was rebuilt. To dignify the seat of local government, the building boasted a portico of four great columns which sheltered a circular case of exterior stairs.

"This effect is so greatly admired," Dr. Caldwell told Alexander with satisfaction, "that already the literary societies of your Alma Mater have copied it." The speaker was himself an alumnus of Chapel Hill.

"I've been touched for a contribution," Alexander confided. "Brother Williamson writes me that the old quadrangle now approaches the Lawn at Charlottesville in beauty, but unfortunately not in wealth. It's passing strange the College should be in need. The material blessings of the Piedmont are in the hands of Presbyterians."

"Who keep the Sabbath day," the Doctor added, "and everything else they get their hands on."

The minister smiled assent.

"And yet," Dr. Caldwell continued, "it isn't only in a material way that Mecklenburg has prospered. Both male and female academies are flourishing, especially the latter under the peculiar genius of your brother Cyrus Johnston, a better preceptor, I think, than preacher. And in spite of endowment difficulties, Davidson College is doing a fine work for our section. Twenty-five years ago we traveled to Chapel Hill for an education or left the State. Today we can keep our sons and our money at home."

"All Presbyterian boys," said Priscilla, "should go to Davidson College, no matter where it is." She knew that the majority of its professors had always been ministers of the gospel and was unimpressed, as were they, by its charter prohibition of sectarian teaching.

"Well, I'm afraid not all Presbyterian boys do," Dr. Caldwell observed. "I intend to send my own there but even sons of our Elders can be found at Chapel Hill. Not only that but Mecklenburgers have patronized almost every college in the North."

"Which accounts, no doubt," Alexander pointed out, "for the struggle our own institutions must make for exist-ence. You don't find a similar disloyalty amongst the New Englanders."

"I understand there are Northern girls at Salem," Pris-cilla remarked.

"The Moravians have an exceptional school," said Dr. Caldwell, "but ever since Camilla Torrance, Mary Ann Irwin and Mary Laura Springs were finished off in Phila-delphia twenty years ago, our daughters have had the idea that the further they roll the brighter the polish."

"That was the Institution de Madame Sazarin," Priscilla remembered. "I used to think I'd send Sarah to Philadel-phia, but if the Lord had spared her my choice now would be one of the seminaries under our own ministers. We have so many excellent ones."

"Not excepting Dr. Johnston's right here at home," added Dr. Caldwell. "And we have also some highly accomplished young ladies. The Public Examinations give evidence that the girls learn how to think as well as memorize. Nor are the social graces neglected. The past May Day celebration was a credit to the sex."

"I'll send up some bachelor deacons next May," laughed Alexander.

"They missed a prime market this year," returned the Doctor. "The 'court' was nonpareil. Octavia Simonton was the student's choice for queen and there have been few in the past as appropriately crowned."

Priscilla wondered what had become of Elizabeth Henderson of 1825, the first belle of the village whose name appeared in public print. How quickly the bloom of beauty faded and how futile were such illusions of happiness. Dear girls, if some one could but warn them of the wages of pride.

Much that modern young ladies accepted as proper Priscilla believed they must eventually reject with sorrow. Dancing schools were available in the village itself, and balls were frequent and festive. Whist parties were pushing out the sewing bee, and fashionable ladies attended the Jockey Club races without apology.

No chit of a girl in 1850 need undergo the soul searching that had been Priscilla's in sitting for a portrait. Many a Mecklenburg physiognomy had been embalmed for posterity by Mr. Mittag. Garl Brown wielded a more flattering brush, and several of the girls prized sketches by members of the artistic Sully family. The wife of Colonel John H. Wheeler, first superintendent of the Mint, was a daughter of the illustrious Thomas himself. As fascinating as portraits, though not always as alluring, were the products of the daguerreotype artists who set up their stands in every Piedmont village.

"Whether for the matrimonial or commercial market," Alexander remarked, "Charlotte's offerings will fail of recognition until the roads are improved." A mired down wagon on Trade or Tryon was as common in '50 as it had been in '25.

"The Plank Road to Salisbury will help," returned his host, "and we are agitating now for a railroad."

"That," observed the Minister with feeling, "is a *desideratum magnissimum*." His clerical dignity had undergone a strain on the Camden-Charlotte Stage which brought him up.

"In spite of our isolation," Dr. Caldwell continued, "these Piedmont settlements have produced some big men. Only last year, as you remember, we could claim both the Governor and the President."

Since both William A. Graham and James Knox Polk were related to Alexander, he remembered very well.

Governor Graham was a son of old General Joseph of Vesuvius Furnace and a grandson of Rural Hill. He was said, in fact, to resemble the builder of the latter more than any other of the prolific patriarch's forty-odd grandsons. Alexander himself owed less in inheritance to this progenitor than to the more remote MacWhorters.

As for President Polk, he was cousin through the Wilsons to everybody in Mecklenburg who was anybody and to many who weren't. The one family that he resembled the least were the fast-living Wilsons themselves.

"We used to argue at Chapel Hill," Dr. Caldwell remarked, unable to resist an allusion to the University's distinction, "whether James Knox Polk or Robert Hall Morrison would be the greatest man. They were very close in scholarship."

Not all Mecklenburgers were admirers of President Polk. James G. Torrance of Cedar Grove would not even permit a Polk weed to grow on his plantation. But though most of the established element were old-line Whigs they could not conceal a touch of pride in the Democratic cousin from Tennessee who had added more territory to the United States than any president since Thomas Jefferson.

Party lines were too closely drawn in Mecklenburg. Distinctions were social as well as political. Only a presumptious Democrat would pay his addresses at the home of a Whig heiress, and only a destitute Whig would accept one.

"I'd as leave marry a Baptist as a Democrat," was attributed to a caustic spinster with more frankness than her fortune warranted.

In ironical humor the Charlotte Hotel advertised that identical accommodations were provided irrespective of party affiliations.

"Even though both were Democrats," Dr. Caldwell observed with reference to Andrew Jackson and the recent incumbent, "two presidents in twenty-five years is not a bad record for a backwoods county."

"Their democracy," the minister smiled, "is doubtless chargeable to their long residence in Tennessee. As well, perhaps, as their elevation to the Presidency." He paused to watch the effect of his shot, and then added thoughtfully.

"It was my fervent prayer that the late great son of the South Carolina Piedmont might do as much for the Union as the men from Mecklenburg."

John Caldwell Calhoun had come of up-country Presbyterian stock but he became the idol and the spokesman as well of the Low-country Episcopalians.

"If there is no compromise this year," Dr. Caldwell observed seriously, "there will be secession or war."

"May God forbid," said Alexander. "Calhoun appeared to me as ready for concessions as Webster. But it will be the task of Henry Clay to reconcile the differences."

"As a Westerner," said Dr. Caldwell, "Clay is in the best position to arbitrate between North and South. I am convinced that the basis of the conflict is the competition between planting and manufacturing. It would have come regardless of slavery and abolition."

"I am inclined to agree," said Alexander. "No Anti-Slavery party has ever attracted a respectable number of Northerners. Immediate emancipation would settle no fundamental differences. We must pray for guidance and light."

The congregation was beginning to assemble. Alexander pulled out his repeater.

"Hadn't you better look over your sermon, dear?" said Priscilla.

"I had, mother," replied her son affectionately. "This is one I've never preached before." He took leave of his host and retired to the Session Room for a final review of his notes.

CHAPTER 28

CLOUD OVER CATAWBA

IN THE CHURCHYARD an Osborne and an Alexander debated in discreet undertones the probable beliefs of the minister. The dialogue did not relate to theology but to history. It was a foregone conclusion that Dr. McIntosh would preach on the Mecklenburg Declaration.

"Since the discovery of the Mecklenburg Resolutions of May 31st," said Osborne, "I wonder if he still holds to the Declaration of May the 20th?"

Controversial agitation of the past dozen years had brought to light copies of Boston, New York and Charleston newspapers which printed in whole or in part a series of Resolutions adopted by Mecklenburg County on May 31, 1775. In these the authority of the King and Parliament was declared annulled and an independent local government provided for the County. But the language of the Resolves was not that of the May 20th declaration as recorded from memory by John McKnitt Alexander. Some contended that the latter were only a confused recollection for the former since no documentary proof was extant for proceedings on the 20th of May.

"There is no mutual exclusiveness in the two," Alexander contended, "Obviously the Resolves only set up a frame of government for the independence declared eleven days before. John McKnitt's notes clearly state that the Committee met again 'after cooling'."

"Then why," Osborne argued, "were only the 31st Resolves printed in the papers of the day?"

"That is not difficult to explain," Alexander answered. "The 31st Resolves were a natural corollary to independence. They amplified the May 20th declaration and offered other localities a precedent for practical procedure. Whether or not Captain James Jack took both documents to Congress in Philadelphia will never be known. As you remember, the North Carolina delegation there told him Mecklenburg's action was 'too premature.' At the time Congress was waving an olive branch of reconciliation at England. No statesman of the time had voiced the rational temerity of the Charlotte patriots."

"I concede you the point," Osborne replied. "Congress would certainly publish nothing of the inflammatory nature of either document, though the newspapers did. But I am still at a loss to reconcile the similarity of the language of the May 20th document with that of Jefferson's masterpiece of July the 4th a year later. To accuse Thomas Jefferson of conscious plagiarism is unthinkable."

"It's thinkable," Alexander retorted, "but unnecessary. The similar phraseology of both was popular parlance before either was written down. Americans didn't begin talking about freedom for the first time in '75, you know. Patrick Henry and others like him in every colony had been arousing the sentiment since the Stamp Act in '65. It remained for Mecklenburg to proclaim it."

"If accepted, you theory obviates the dilemma nicely," Osborne assented. "Otherwise we'd be forced to impugn either the mental faculties of your ancestor or the moral integrity of Thomas Jefferson. I prefer to do neither. I'm surprised the explanation did not occur to John Adams, although he would doubtless have concealed it to irritate Jefferson."

"We don't have to depend on the opinions of John Adams," Alexander rejoined tartly. "He knew no more about it than Jefferson. A great deal occurred beyond the bounds of Massachusetts and Virginia that their historians have not recorded."

"Agreed," said Osborne, "And whether there was one paper or two seems of no great significance to me. There was nothing in '75 as advanced as Mecklenburg action of either the 20th or the 31st."

"Your last statement is correct," said Alexander. "Your first the result of your Iredell County provincialism. If you Osbornes had lived three miles south you'd have seen more light."

Osborne gave a good-natured chuckle. "In our arguments over details we have lost sight of essentials. Charlotte's example undoubtedly encouraged wavering patriots and influenced our Provincial Congress to adopt its resolution of April 12th in '76."

"Yes," said Alexander, "it was no accident that the North Carolina delegation to Congress was the first to be instructed to work for independence. Without May the 20th there would have been no April the 12th."

"Let's say without May '75," Osborne suggested. "For that matter, December 25th remains to be verified by Biblical scholars. It's events, not dates, that make history."

The opening chords of the melodeon ended their colloquy and each authority entered the church confirmed by his arguments in his own beliefs.

Dr. McIntosh did not fail his people. Like most men with roots in the Catawba Valley he entertained few doubts on the 20th of May. Much of the voluminous literature which had appeared in defense of that document had come from the pens of Presbyterian ministers. Were not nine of the twenty-seven signers known to be Ruling Elders of that denomination and the remainder members in good standing? Was not the Reverend Hezekiah James Balch of Poplar Tent the John Witherspoon of Mecklenburg's immortality?

Alexander took his text from Deuteronomy, the 32nd chapter, the seventh verse:

> Remember the days of old, consider the years of many generations: Ask thy father and he will show thee, thy elders and they will tell thee.

The preacher was a Daniel come to judgment. Mecklenburg had asked its fathers and its elders. It chose to believe what they told. In the absence of written records only the years of many generations stood as proof. Everyone knew that the original documents had been burned in the house of John McKnitt Alexander. The old secretary's word was as good as his bond.

"Remember the days of old." Here was a Biblical injunction for the celebration of May the 20th. Could a God fearing people do otherwise? Dr. McIntosh was a man after Mecklenburg's own heart.

Priscilla made no effort to take her eyes from the face of her son. He stood in the high pulpit dedicated to the greatest of all callings and it was no sin to feast one's eyes on the prophet of the Lord. His sonorous voice, his eloquent periods, his restrained but moving gestures filled her heart with joy.

"No woman," she breathed silently, "has been more blessed since Elizabeth the mother of John." Then hastily a prayer: "Dear Lord, if that be a sacrilege, forgive it."

What happiness would be hers to live near her son, to hear his voice from the pulpit on every consecrated Sabbath. In the South Carolina village the ladies had come to call to tell her the good her son had done for their town.

They knew her only as the mother of their beloved pastor. For them there was no Priscilla's Price, this millstone which hung about her neck on a chain forged by pride.

"Not my will, oh Lord, but thine be done," she whispered resolutely. Only God could sever the links of her chain. Her debt was not yet paid.

Alexander expounded his text to include the struggle of the early Presbyterians of the upcountry for freedom of worship. The tidewater Episcopalians had confined Mecklenburg and Rowan Counties to the ecclesiastical boundaries of St. Luke's Parish. But no rector took up his glebe, despite the establishment of the Anglican Church by public tax. Calvinistic elders were chosen vestrymen by the "parishioners" and tithes were paid to the church of their own persuasion.

"Our forefathers," Alexander said, "may or may not have believed the tenets of Episcopacy heretical. That was not the issue at stake. Not how shall we believe, but who shall determine our beliefs. There was no alternative to independence."

A murmur of concerted applause ran through the congregation. Many had wayward offspring who had found the graces of Episcopalians matrimonially irresistible. It would not do to be too hard on their theology. Their politics was a different matter.

To illuminate his postulate, Alexander cited historical examples:

"The first missionaries of our faith in the Piedmont defied the Crown in order to give our fathers a Presbyterian marriage; the Reverend Alexander Craighead shook the dust of Pennsylvania from his feet and set up his stand under the free oaks of the Catawba Valley; the trustees

of Queens College rejected the blandishments of the Anglican Tories and conducted their school without a charter
according to the dictates of their consciences."

Alexander reviewed the representative features of Presbyterian government. There was no hierarchy of popes and
bishops but moderators in rotation. These were elected
by ministers and elders chosen by the people. The Constitution of the United States owed much to the systemics of
the Calvinists.

> Remember the days of old, consider the years of
> many generations: Ask thy father and he will
> show thee, thy elders and they will tell thee.

To the congregation, Alexander spoke as one inspired.
His was the gift of tongues to voice the mind of Mecklenburg. The tautness of Presbyterian responses relaxed. Gone
was any lingering resentment at the pomp and circumstances of his birth. Priscilla's Price might belong to his
family, but Dr. McIntosh belonged to the Church.

After the sermon, half the congregation filed by to give
the minister the right hand of fellowship. Priscilla decided
to wait and see him later. She might have stood by his side
but her spirit was content to know that he was hers.

As she walked out alone she received the congratulations
of many who remained in their pews. In the aisle acquaintances of all degrees stopped to kiss her cheek or
press her hand. There was no malice behind these smiles.
Her pathway was strewn with palm leaves.

"My cup runneth over." Wistfully she remembered
Alexander's pleas that she make her home near him. But
the vista of bright hope was blocked by a wall of Flemish
bond and Grecian columns.

"God has already blessed me beyond my deserts."

Priscilla had learned resignation. Like her Biblical namesake she longed to become "a helper in Jesus Christ," though for her life there was to be no Aquila "much in the Lord with the church that is in their house."

When she stepped out into the yard her eyes caught the dejected figure of Scipio under a large elm. He motioned convulsively toward her. Tears were streaming down his shiny black face.

"What is it, Scipio?" She hastened to him. "Tell me what has happened?"

Great sobs shook his frame as he spoke.

"Missus," he said, "Lord bless you, Missus. Our house done burnt down."

Priscilla was struck with a tingling like a shock from lightning. For a moment she was speechless.

"Was anyone hurt," she asked.

"No'm," Scipio sobbed, "warn't nobody there. We didn't git nothin' out. We was holdin' the sunrise prayer meetin' in the quarters. Nobody minded no noise o' fire. Eben de walls done fell in. Lord Jesus, Missus, it's done gone to glory."

He sat on the ground and wept.

"Mr. Alexander and I will go back with you as soon as he comes out." Priscilla's voice had a far-away tone. "Don't feel too badly, Scipio. God does all things for the best."

The congregation had left the church. A few stood about under the trees. The Carsons, Springs' and Irwins were making their way to their carriages. There was nothing unusual about a mistress talking to her colored driver and Priscilla and Scipio had conversed unnoticed.

As she walked back toward the church, Priscilla was

stopped by the Reverend Robert Hall Morrison who had come in from Cottage Home for the service.

"Cousin Priscilla," he said, "the spirit of the Lord is upon your son. God has greatly blessed you."

A feeling of serenity suffused Priscilla. For the first time since the death of her daughter the peace for which she had striven was completely hers.

"Thank you, Cousin Robert." There were tears in Priscilla's eyes. "I think the Lord will forgive me if I am proud of my son."

She did not move when Dr. Morrison left her. For a moment she closed her eyes. Billowing smoke from the crash of Priscilla's Price enveloped her consciousness. Suddenly a gust from the heavens blew aside the darkness. In the stillness after storm a clean hilltop shown brightly.

The shadow of the cloud over Catawba passed forever from Priscilla's heart.